LUCY V HAY is an author and script editor for movies and short film. A teenage mum herself, she grew frustrated with the 'usual' narratives about this subject. She decided to challenge these outdated stereotypes and assumptions by telling her own experience, as well as her friends' as pregnant teenagers and young parents.

She lives in Devon, UK, with her husband, three children, five cats and some Great African Land Snails.

Lucy V Hay

PROOF POSITIVE

Littwitz PRESS

COPYRIGHT

Littwitz Press
Dahl House, Brookside Crescent
Exeter EX4 8NE

First published in Great Britain by Bang2Write in 2014

www.littwitzpress.com

A CIP catalogue record for this book is available
from the British Library.

ISBN: 978-1-9998552-9-1

To all pregnant teens out there ...
Whatever you choose, it will be okay. You got this.

To any young parents reading this ...
You're doing great. You are not alone.

*'It is our choices that show what we really are,
far more than our abilities.'*
J.K. Rowling

Prologue

First, the line to show it worked. Then, a second one: faint, but very definitely there. *Oh my God.*

Pregnant.

I sat staring at the tester stick. My brain could not catch up. There must be some kind of mistake? I'd had unprotected sex, sure, but *it had only been the once*. People had to try for years normally! They'd go on special diets; have to take up exercise; not wear tight pants (!); even get laboratory help.

But oh no, not me.

I'd literally had to try my hardest at everything I'd ever done before now … Study like mad for tests? *Check.* Take three separate auditions for the netball team? *Check.* It had even taken me about twenty goes to climb the rope ladder into our old tree house! But this?

First time: score!

I couldn't be *that* pregnant. I'd had no morning sickness or cravings, though I'd had my suspicions. I felt somehow… *different.* There was a metallic taste in my mouth and my small boobs felt about three times bigger. They hurt like hell, too. But I'd told myself, over and over: *You can't be.* I mean, I couldn't be that unlucky … Right??

Yet here I was.

I'd had to walk right to the other side of town, to the other pharmacy, to buy the test. The other one fulfilled my mother's many prescriptions. (In my paranoid mind, I could see Mr. Edwards going straight to the phone… 'Mrs. Carmichael? Your Lizzie's been in… Buying a PREGNANCY TEST.') Pharmacists don't have to take an oath of confidentiality like doctors… Do they?

I'd taken it right away, unable to wait the forty-minute bus ride back home. I had to do it right there and then. So, there I was, pregnancy tester in a hand, seated in a rank, foul-smelling public toilet. It had slit windows and ultra-violet light, its graffittied door and walls shouting out various slogans: WANT LESBIAN SEX? CALL 788996. IF YOU'RE READING THIS, YOU'RE A BITCH. KATIE DORRIGAN IS A SLAG.

Nice.

Panic struck me, my heart hammered. It felt like it might burst out of my chest, like in cartoons. What was I supposed to do? How was I supposed to feel about this? I had zero clue. This felt too big for me.

Thoughts clambered through in my head. I'd never been against having kids, but obviously the thought of having one *right now* terrified me. There were so many things I'd thought I would do first! Go to university. Go travelling. Live with my best friend, Shona. Get away from this dump of a town, have a career. Just the usual stuff. I want to do what young people do… just because they do. No special reason. Was this what I was destined to be now: someone's mum before I had I even been me?

I stood up to leave the grotty toilet cubicle but sat down again. I couldn't face the world outside. I tried to pull myself together, empty my brain. But random images and thoughts kept creeping their way in, uninvited.

I could already see my mother's face, pinched tight in that particular way of hers: 'Oh Lizzie.' She would simply sigh, though her meaning would be clear: *I'm very disappointed in you. I thought you were supposed to be bright?*

I could see all five of my sisters, eyes wide, at least one of them delighted I had fallen from grace with such a bump.

I could see Mike, hands dug in his pockets in that way of his, but also Mike's dad, Francis. His slack face, his yellow teeth clamped on his pipe, puffing away his disapproval. Mike's dad had never liked me (that was okay, I didn't like him either).

But all this would be fine… Right? Because this was just about logistics. Inconvenient. Scary. But I would be okay. Because I had Mike; Mike loved me. He and I could decide what to do. We would work this out. Together.

But I didn't move.

I sat there for what felt like hours, though looking at my watch only twenty minutes passed. Time seemed to slow down within those toilets. I was struck by the silence. I could hear nothing of the marketplace beyond; the shouting of stallholders, trying to offload their stock. No one came into the toilets. There was no creak of rusty door hinges; no splash in the wet patch around the sinks; no blare of the hand dryer.

I stood on the closed toilet seat. I stretched towards the thin, lead-laced window next to the filthy, suspended cistern. I saw the shadows of people's feet on the pavement above, moving past the glass in the street above. It was like peering through a dirty fish tank. Movement was snatched away; then it swam up against the glass, then it was gone again.

I was alone in the world.

I sat back down on the closed toilet seat. I knew that the moment I went outside, everything would rush in at me, become real. Everyone would be in my face. I'd have to deal with what others would throw at me. Accusations. Demands. Disappointments. So many people were going to judge me, people I cared about. And even those I didn't care about were still going to talk about me and somehow that made me suddenly care about what they were going to say.

I closed my eyes. An image swam into my brain: me and Shona at her house, drunk on vodka again. We'd been singing eighties classics at the top of our lungs watching an oldies music channel. Her mother had been sleeping upstairs, whacked out on antidepressants while Shona's father was away on 'business'. A neighbour had come around shouting. Shona's mother had staggered downstairs and yelled at him, swaying from left to right on her bare feet. Shona and I stood there eyeballing the neighbour too, forcing down laughter until the door was closed. We'd erupted as soon as the latch clicked. Shona's mother paused on the stairs. She regarded us with that puzzled look of hers before taking herself off to bed again in her two-hundred-pound negligee.

Another image whirled into my thoughts: an old teacher of mine, Mrs. Jenkin. 'Jenkin, NO S!' she would always bark (so obviously we'd always called her 'Mrs. Jenkin-No-S' behind her back - plus once to her face too by accident. She'd simply laughed). She was your typical hippy-dippy English teacher-type. She'd wear long skirts and scarves, as well as thousands of bracelets and strings of beads. She dyed her hair bright red, even though she was really old, easily fifty. She'd died of cancer the year we'd taken our GCSEs. But even though she was ill, she came in to as many classes as she could.

'You have your exams.' She said and a part of me admired her, even though she was a teacher.

Mrs Jenkin-No-S died the same week we sat our papers. It was like she'd delivered us as far as she could go and then was gone herself. Just like that. I'd never liked English much before, but Mrs. Jenkin-No-S had changed all that for me. I guess seeing someone so passionate for her subject was infectious or something. I found myself actually looking at the websites she recommended or checking the school library for the plays and novels she raved about.

'What's the difference between the Big Bang and Hiroshima?'

Mrs. Jenkin-No-S enquired this one lesson (before I'd realised she was actually cool). Her question had something to do with the text we were reading that term, but then Shona kicked me under the table at that exact moment.

I shot up in my chair with a squeal. A snicker went through the class like a Mexican wave. Mrs. Jenkin-No-S's sights set on me, her thin lips pursed in a snake-like smile.

'Elizabeth,' she'd said (she never called me Lizzie), 'Would you like to share your thoughts?'

Not really. Panic lanced through me. Big Bang? Hiroshima? What the hell was this mad old bird going on about!

'One was the creation of the universe… and the other destroyed everything?' I winced, sure this was the wrong answer.

'Exactly!' Mrs. Jenkin-No-S exclaimed, banging her book down on the desk with a slam. 'There is NO difference.'

Shona made a *cuckoo* gesture and shot daggers at me, wanting me to shut up. For some reason, though I listened to Shona most of the time, I chose not to that day.

'Um, I thought I said there was loads of difference?' My voice was timid, but clear. 'Like, opposite ends of the scale?'

There was a titter throughout the class. Great. Now everyone thought I was a complete freak.

But Mrs. Jenkin smiled and for a moment I forgot the rest of the class. It was just me and her. I'd never felt like that before. Always at home, it was a massive competition between us all: *notice me, love me, watch me*! At school too, there was just a mad melee of faces and names. The ones who were bad stood out the most; the rest of us faded away to nothing. I'd heard one of Mum's friends, Nora, a teacher, say once: *How do we remember the names of everyone in our classes? We don't – we only remember the troublemakers'*!

But in that moment, Mrs. Jenkin-No-S saw me. *Actually saw me.*

Then the spell was broken. I became aware again of the glares of the others in the class. The contemptuous sneer of Helen Billimore to my left drew my gaze. Embarrassed, I averted my eyes.

'They're both explosions. The only difference is…' Mrs. Jenkin-No-S paused for effect, '…The outcome.'

A kind of collective sigh rippled through the class: the teenagers in the room figured the only adult in the room was going senile. But Mrs. Jenkin-No-S didn't seem to let that bother her. Though I didn't want to, I found myself rolling my eyes with the rest of them. I was annoyed to see Mrs. Jenkin still regarding me with those beady eyes of hers when I snuck another look at her.

'Crazy old cow.' Shona muttered.

I mumbled an almost soundless agreement. Back then, guilt blossomed inside me for a reason I couldn't quite understand.

But now, I knew why: Mrs. Jenkin-No-S was right. Hundreds of thousands of girls and women take this same test every single day, yet how it works out is always different. Pregnant. Congratulations or commiserations: what is the outcome? For some, there will be a happy ending; for others no such fairy tale. Some will have no ending at all.

What was it going to be, for me? What could it be?

I wanted to go and tell Mrs. Jenkin my news, ask her what I should do. But obviously, I couldn't. She'd been gone nearly three years now. I'd read about her death in the paper and seen the announcement for her funeral. Shona declared we should go, make sure the old cow was really dead.

'Knowing her, she'll come out the grave like a frigging bright red vampire!'

Shona threw her blonde hair back as she guffawed, like it was the funniest joke in the world. In that moment, I'd hated my best friend. But I'd just clenched my fists and mumbled she was morbid. I'd managed to distract with the idea we should go out; see if we could get served at The Moon, the main pub in town. Shona had immediately thought that was a better idea. Between the possibility of alcohol and causing a ruck, there was never any contest – even for Shona. I'd felt relieved I could distract her so easily and keep her away from Mrs. Jenkin-No-S' family. 'Cos she must have had a family, right? I wondered whether she had a daughter or son, or both. Did they miss her? What would the baby inside of me right now think of me, one day?

Baby. Whoa.

I'd been so busy trying to digest the word 'pregnant' into my psyche, it was hard to believe the situation actually meant something else too. *There was another person inside me.* Or was there? I couldn't decide.

Panic struck me all over again. I tried to concentrate on something else, empty my mind of accusatory faces. I recalled a sleepover with Shona. We were about eleven; we'd just met in our new class at 'big' school. We were two outsiders: she was fat, I wore glasses. Two outcasts should be together, it just made sense. There were kids more extra than us. As long as we stayed out the way of the cool kids, everything would be fine. So, me and Shona became BFFs, because without each other we would have no one.

That first weekend of our new school, we had a sleepover at Shona's house. We made our very first pitcher of orange juice and filled it full of vodka from Shona's father's drinks cabinet, thinking he would never notice (he never did, either). Shona's family was rich (at least, in comparison to mine). Shona even had her own en suite bathroom, with a heated towel rail and the hot water was *on all day*. I was in awe: at my house, if you didn't get up early, even at weekends, the hot water would be gone.

To me, Shona's life was almost like being a princess. In a house with six girls under eighteen, there were never any biscuits in the barrel, or clean knickers. Our little country cottage was besieged by mice. We couldn't afford central heating. In winter the house was so cold, the sheets on the bed felt wet and there was a constant tang of damp in the air. Water was provided by a huge tank and pump, prone to leaking. One year I got out of bed to discover my bedroom was flooded right up to my ankles.

The electricity would go off at our house – and stay off. We were the company's last priority out in the arse end of nowhere. My mother had to keep big pots of candles and matches on the sideboard all year round, 'just in case'. Every winter the patio would disappear under water as the nearby river burst its banks. Once, my twin sisters Clare and Charlotte could have been killed when a huge piece of the roof fell onto their beds (luckily, they'd been having a sleepover in the living room, with two friends).

Escaped animals from nearby farms would invade us on a regular basis, too. Cows and sheep mostly, though once my mother went out to pick some flowers and came in white-faced. After gulping down a glass of water, she reported there was a vulture sitting in the crab apple tree. We thought she'd lost her mind. But we'd gone to investigate and sure enough, there he was, sitting halfway up the tree (he was much bigger than I expected). A few phone calls later revealed he'd given his handler the slip at the local wildlife park. That was our life.

So, I felt like I'd won the lottery at Shona's: I must have stayed in her shower for twenty whole minutes. The familiar thud in my chest sounded as I got out, but no one shouted at me. It was brilliant. Later, we drank the vodka and streamed movies, chatting like we'd known each other forever. I was struck by how peaceful it was at her house. There was no shouting, no arguing, no slamming doors. Yet weirdly, in that moment I felt just a tiny bit homesick.

But my attention was diverted whilst we were watching some lame film about a time-travelling guy, when a drunken Shona opened up and shared her oddball theory:

'I think some moments are meant to be,' Shona declared, 'You can't change them. Other stuff can only change around them.'

My brain fuzzy from alcohol, I didn't realise she was actually being serious. I would come to know Shona didn't do that much: she reckoned everything was always 'a joke' or 'tedious'. But back then, I'd known her just a few days. It would be years before I would have the full picture of what Shona was really like: sensationalist, slutty, self-loathing, all wrapped up in a desperate bid to get her parents to notice her.

'Like it's written in the stars?' I giggled.

'Nope,' Shona huffed, 'nothing cheesy like that. I just think some moments happen and you can't undo them, you know? But from there - that single starting point - *anything* can happen.'

'But doesn't that mean we're not in control?' I enquired.

'We all have choices,' Shona said with surprising authority for an eleven-year-old school girl.

'But how does it work?' I was genuinely confused. 'If there are some things that we have to do and others we choose to do, how can that make sense?'

'Life doesn't make sense.'

'That sounds like a cop out to me.'

'Not a cop out,' Shona countered, 'a paradox.'

We'd carried on drinking. The next day I'd had my first ever hangover, waking in a pool of vomit. Shona's mother had taken one look at me and freaked out, sure I was dying. She drove me to The General, Shona in the front seat, arms folded, face like thunder. She'd told her mother I was fine but had taken it personally when her mum had not taken her word for it. When the doctor had informed Shona's mother I would be fine as long as I drank plenty of fluids – 'only not the type of fluids she had last night' – Shona's mother finally clicked and called *my* mother.

Mum had arrived in her rusty little car, parking outside Shona's parents' fancy townhouse. I'd nearly died of shame when my incredibly pregnant Mum got out of the car and I saw she was still wearing her pyjamas. She hadn't had the twins yet, back then. She was a massive, full-on beached whale cliché; how she even fit behind the steering wheel was beyond me. Even worse, Amanda, Sal and Hannah were crammed in the back seat looking like lost woodland elves. I was sure they'd backcombed their hair just to show me up.

But Shona's Mother pretended not to notice, which was good of her. As our mothers chatted idly, I wondered if Shona had ever had to make believe she actually wanted to be 'different' to everyone else. What was it like to have a choice?

'Dad could have picked me up.' I clambered into the passenger seat, next to Mum. Her elbow was practically in my ribs as she yanked back the gearstick.

'You know Dad's not here at the moment.' Disapproval radiated off Mum like lava off a volcano. It was going to take me ages to work my way back into her good books again.

'When's he coming back?' I demanded.

'Don't start, Lizzie.' Mum said, automatically.

Immediately my little sisters started chanting, *'Don't start, Lizzie! Don't start!'* Sal reached through the gap in the seats and pinched me. I reached back and tried to pinch her. Suddenly a fight broke out: Hannah was crying; Amanda's shrieking that hideous laugh of hers; whilst Sal's telling me what a loser I am and how she wishes I was dead.

'Now look what you've started!' Mum hollered at me as the car swept past endless fields.

Oh God, Sal and Amanda. I felt a sense of dread pierce my heart. What were they going to say? There was just three and a half years between us eldest Carmichael girls … Yet it might as well be three million. It was always one rule for Sal and Amanda, another for the rest of us. I could never quite work out if those two were Mum's favourites, or if she'd realised that by giving them a wide berth, her life became easier. Maybe both.

Sal was fifteen now, ploughing through her exams. We all had to be on best behaviour, of course. Always, 'be quiet, Sal's studying'; 'don't disturb your sister'; 'Sal works very hard.' Sal The Genius. I didn't remember Mum ever sounding the fanfare for my exams. I was always praised for my efforts, but it was clear there were inverted commas involved: *Yes, Lizzie is a good girl but she's only doing the 'creative arts'.* Not real subjects. Thanks Mum.

As for Amanda… She did nothing at all, yet somehow managed to opt out of the blame for anything. She'd limped her way through a handful of exams without even trying. She was now coasting her way through a beauty course at college, but 'you know what Amanda's like,' as Mum would say. Yes, not a care in the world because no one puts anything on her. Ever.

Why can't that be me?

Back in the toilets, the acrid stench of piss, stagnant water and old air freshener came rushing in at me. I couldn't keep stalling. My time was up.

Resolute, I stood up, grabbing my bag. I undid the lock on the cubicle door, walking towards the sinks. For some reason, I couldn't bring myself to throw the tester in the overflowing bin with all the manky hand towels. Instead I undid my college bag and slipped it inside.

I looked in the mirror. Looking at the aluminium glass,

my face was little more than a blur. I had to peer right in to make out my features. When I did, I was struck by how young I looked … But I was. Just one short week away from eighteen, days away from my A Level results. The eve of my adult life, yet here I was: *Baby Mama*. I noted how puffy and red my eyes were. I'd been crying and hadn't even known it. My eyeshadow had smeared on the left-hand side of my cheek. I grabbed another rough hand towel and wet it, rubbing as hard as I can. The worst of the smear was gone. It would do.

How could this have happened? I wasn't dim. I knew sex could mean babies! But somehow, I'd never thought this would be me. Teen mums were the ones you saw on chat shows, rowing with their equally young partners about who the dad was. They were the type of girls with too much make up, a ton of gold-plated jewellery and sweat pants.

Weren't they?

A strange sort of calm settled over me. I couldn't put this off any longer. I had to do something. I had to go home, tell my parents, tell Mike, even my sisters. Perhaps eleven-year-old Shona was right? Perhaps this was one of those moments I couldn't change. Perhaps this had always been part of my plan. Whether that meant pre-destined or part of the unconscious choices I had already made, it didn't matter: it would be there, no matter what I chose to do.

But what next?

Sal

*'Sister is probably the most competitive relationship
in the family, but once the sisters are grown, it becomes
the strongest.'*
Margaret Mead

One

My mobile rang.

The noise pierced the silence inside the toilets. I was filled with a sense of urgency. I simply had to answer, which was not like me. I'd purposefully not downloaded many apps; I preferred to check most of my social media on the aged old laptop at home. It also gave me the perfect excuse to be out of range. With regular signal so poor where we lived, it meant Mum couldn't call me via Wi-Fi, or send me eleventy billion messages on every available platform going. I did have Snapchat but like most grown-ups, she didn't get how to use that, so I was safe. With a mother like mine, you had to think ahead.

But I felt totally unable to let the phone ring and ring. I normally kept my phone in my pocket, but not today. It was at the bottom of my bag. I scrabbled about in vain, then chucked the bag on the counter next to the sinks. The light of the LCD reflected off a pencil tin, a book, yet still I was unable to locate it.

Then, just as my hand touched the plastic case of the completely non-state of the art phone, it obviously stopped ringing. I swore under my breath. I grabbed it up anyway, looking at the screen. 'MISSED CALL – SAL'.

Confusion swirled through my head. What the hell was Sal calling me for? She went out of her way to not even speak to me, unless it was to insult me. Whether it was the fact I (apparently) looked like a tart in a new dress I had saved for; the B that 'could have been an A'; or just the usual idea I was a complete loser, Sal had the dark skills to make me feel like crap, day in, day out.

But then the phone rang in my hand again: there was Sal's name, flashing. I hesitated. Did I really want to talk to my little sister? She could be such a bitch. I could already imagine the curl of her sneering upper lip, her rolling eyes. Inside me, despair turned to anger. Shouldn't Sal have been looking up to me? Why did she have to put me down every chance she got? Why couldn't I have a normal life!

After three or four more rings, I pressed the green button, placing the phone to my ear at last. 'Hello?'

'Finally!' Sal said, 'Forgotten how to answer a phone, have you?'

I gritted my teeth. 'I was busy.'

'Join the club.' Sal said, competing with me as always. 'I need some note cards for my revision.'

'So?' I was being pathetic; I knew full well what she was asking.

'Mum said you would still probably be in town.'

Her secret weapon: *Mum said, Mum said...* Whatever Sal wanted: whether it was note cards for her revision, to say whatever she liked or to eat dinner in her room while the rest of us had to sit at the table, Sal could somehow magically rely on Mum to back her up, even indirectly. Well, screw that, today of all days.

'I don't have any money.' I could feel the clank of loose change in my jacket pocket. *I need it for the bus*, I justified to myself.

There was a short pause. 'Are you alright?' Sal said.

I almost gasped, I was that surprised. I honestly couldn't remember a time Sal had asked me that question. If I ever felt ill? I was a hypochondriac. If I ever felt sad? I was an idiot. Sal believed all creative people liked to be miserable for the sake of their art, making us all by virtue a bunch of losers. Whenever I'd tried to talk about my excitement about going to university, she'd cut the conversation dead. As far as she was concerned, I would be messing about for three years. So, perhaps it was that sense of shock at her actually seeming to care for once, that prompted me to blurt out:

'I'm pregnant.'

There was more dead silence on the other end of the line. For one terrible moment I thought she'd gone to get Mum. *Oh, shit!* My breath caught in my throat; nausea flooded through me. I hadn't wanted it to come out like this, not over the bloody phone. *Why had I just done that??*

'Are you still there?' I said, with trepidation.

'I'm thinking.' Sal replied tersely.

'What's there to think about?' My voice cracked. Not for the first time that morning, I found myself on the brink of freaking out: 'It's not you it's happening to, it's me!'

As soon as I said the words, I regretted them. I'd raised my voice. Sal could turn on a hair trigger and I'd just given her a full-on invite to rain down the pain in her usual devastating style. But for once, Sal didn't.

'Where are you?'

'In the marketplace.' I gulped.

'I'm going to get the bus now.' Sal said. 'I'll meet you, wait there. I'll be as quick as I can.'

And with that, she rang off.

Two

I just stood there, staring at the phone like an idiot. What had just happened? Had my little sister – *the one who was always at great pains to tell me how much she hated me –* just said she was going to lend me her support? Was she really on her way? For the first time that day, a kind of hope pierced my heart. Perhaps I had been wrong all these years? Maybe Sal loved me after all.

I wandered out of the toilets. As I predicted, real life hit me full-on. The sun was high in the sky. It was early afternoon, peak time at the market.

The hustle and bustle seemed larger than usual, faces looming in on me. The shouts of the traders mingled with the haggling of the customers. The waft of raw meat from the butcher's stall, fillets packed in ice at the fishmonger's. Two pitches full of brightly-coloured hippy clothes and bags. An old woman touted for business from her trestle table full of junk: flowerpots, tarnished silver jewellery, old books that smelt mouldy. A mum pushed her homemade wares: jam, cards and other trinkets. There was a toddler sitting next to her, in a pushchair.

I stopped next to the mum's stall to look at the child. A little boy of perhaps two years old, he was shaded from the sun. I could tell this boy had been on the market his whole life. He had a little lunchbox with robots on; there was a collection of books and jigsaw puzzles in the tray underneath his pushchair. From the handle bars a nappy bag hung, no doubt filled with whatever else he needed.

In-between serving customers, his mum would give him her attention – squeezing his cheeks, stroking his arm or talking to him – and the child would respond with a huge smile, meant just for her.

Watching the two of them together, the turmoil in my mind stopped racing for a few minutes. That mum had to be just like me: she was creative, but she hadn't let having a baby stop her. She had followed her dream, making her cards and jam and trinkets – and taken baby too. Why couldn't I do the same? Perhaps I could follow the same path. Or perhaps, just perhaps, I could go to university anyway and take my baby with me?

Then Sal arrived. In that razor-sharp way of hers, she took one look at me and where my gaze was heading, towards the child.

'Not here.' She said.

We walked through the marketplace in silence towards the park: to the broken, graffittied bandstand where the problem teens gathered every night to drink cider. Back with urban deprivation, seeing the cracked glass in the panes, I felt my bubble burst. Even the sight of children beyond the bandstand in the small play park did nothing to lift my spirits. They were there with their own young mothers, all sweat pants and bling, the kind I had always been certain I would never be.

Finally, Sal opened her mouth. 'You can't have it.'

A dreadful sinking feeling heaped itself on me. I could see the truth of Sal's words. It had been in the back of my mind the whole time, struggling to be heard as I tried to tell myself an alternative route was possible.

I was barely eighteen. I had no money and no prospect of making any. Babies were expensive, this child would have nothing. Mike would not want to know, I knew that deep down. My own family could not support me, for they had no money either. It would be unfair on me, unfair on the child and unfair on my family to follow this pregnancy through.

Yet still the rebellious heart of my relationship with Sal tried to beat. I attempted to disagree: 'I'd manage.'

'On what?' Sal eyeballed me, her expression grim.

The question hung in the air like cigarette smoke. I knew what she was really asking. I knew there was government help available for girls in my position and so did Sal. Our own mother had used it. Life had been an uphill struggle for her, raising all six of us; it still was. But money was available if I could swallow my pride and fill in the forms and live with less. The child would have to make do, too. The real question Sal was asking was, 'Did I want the same life as our mother's?' though neither of us had the guts to say it aloud.

'You're going to university next month.' Sal said.

'I'd manage.' I repeated, dogged as ever.

'Everyone would talk about you,' Sal continued, determined. 'You'd have no friends, no boyfriends. You'd just be the 'pregnant one'. Then for the next two years you'd have a crying baby and studies to do, you'd be all alone.'

'I don't care.' I whispered.

'You'd have no money and there's no guarantee when you get out of university you'll even end up in a job related to your degree. You'll have loads of debt, but you won't even be able to pick and choose jobs to get by because you'll need a babysitter. Bar work will be out, no childminders or nurseries work past six o' clock. You wouldn't be able to do weekends…!'

'I don't have to go to university.' I said.

'You want to go to university.' Sal countered.

There was no real arguing with that. I'd been dreaming of going to the big city for months. Away from nowheresville where we lived, I really felt my dreams could come true. I had seen the studios at my university, the potter's wheels, the resources on offer – and I wanted them. Desperately. But:

'There are other ways.' I found myself saying, 'Maybe I could go later, when the kid's at school? There's a child on the market, with his mum, they're doing fine!'

Then Sal delivered her most devastating blow. 'She probably has a husband at home, earning the big bucks … It's probably just a hobby to her.'

Pain and disappointment coursed through me. I knew Sal was right. But stilll couldn't accept my sister's words.

'I could manage.' I said again.

And that was it: compassionate Sal was gone. Judgemental Sal returned, eyes blazing. Perhaps from her point of view she felt I was dismissing her good advice, saying it was not good enough? But Sal, despite her large IQ, was still only fifteen. She could not truly understand what I was going through, without having faced the same herself.

'So ruin your life.' She declared.

Stung, I watched Sal stalk off, away from the bandstand. I wanted to call her back but didn't. Pride would not allow me to back down. Resentment flowed through my veins: *who did Sal think she was? She was just a kid.*

Then with a jolt and a lurching of my stomach, I realised: *So am I.*

Three

I couldn't go home right away. Riding on the same bus as Sal, in silence, was too much. So, I wandered blindly back into town, bypassing the market and back into its broken-down old high street.

When I'd been a small child, I had seen only the sea stretching out bright beyond the town: the pebbled beach, the donkeys tethered to the promenade railings. On the lampposts of the sea front, coloured bunting was tied and lights flashed and bells rang in the arcades. I had thought I was the luckiest little girl in the world. Living near the seaside was a dream to so many, yet I was living it.

Gulls soared up from the old promenade and its ancient neon arcades. They hovered above the faded posters, broken windows, the hastily-scrawled graffiti. Back when Queen Victoria had been on the throne, this town had been a luxurious resort, the type of place where only the privileged holidayed. It had been a jewel of the north coast. Now, it was decayed and sad, forgotten as Brits went abroad on cheap package deals instead. Undervalued by its locals, most were able only to work during the summer months as its few B&Bs, hotels and family attractions closed down in winter.

This place was a dump. It would never change, either. That was the problem: house prices were high as city-folk descended at weekends and summer holidays. They bought the lie: it was all cream teas and Famous Five. They never saw the metal shutters go up in winter, or the dead streets of the ghost town. For every rich family like Shona's, tucked away from 'real' town on huge red brick and sandstone estates, there were ten more families like mine, scraping by at best. We were not living our own lives at all, but some marketer's stereotypical dream of seaside living. But only those with money could buy into it. The rest of us were left with the scraps.

I had to get out.

Sal's words kept rolling around and around in my head: *'You'll be the pregnant one… You'd be all alone.'*

I couldn't leave and take the baby with me. But I couldn't stay and raise a child in a place like this. I had seen too many people's lives go to waste here: they struggled to get by, never finding enough work, always doing without. The sadness in the women's eyes, the frustration in the men's; the unspoken resentment that bubbled under the surface in this place. There was only one answer: Sal was right.

I couldn't have this baby.

Hot tears pricked my eyelids as I stared vacantly into shop windows, looking at my haunted reflection, rather than the goods beyond the glass. I never wanted this! I never wanted to be *that* girl. The slut. The stupid one.

The baby killer.

There had been a girl called Vanessa in Year Nine at school. She was all round edges: moon-like face, rotund middle, large boobs. One day, halfway through the academic year, she had just disappeared. The rumour machine was in full swing before break time, but shreds of truth got through.

It was said Vanessa got pregnant by Shane Dawkins, that eighteen-year-old arsehole who hung around the school gates. He really fancied himself and hoped little thirteen and fourteen-year-olds would too. He wasn't wrong, either: with his cigarettes and booze, he must have seemed sophisticated and cool. Row after row of girls were used and discarded by him. Vanessa had been just one of many. She'd gone to him and told him she was pregnant, but he and his squad had just laughed at her, Shona had reported with wide eyes.

That night, Vanessa had gone home and taken twenty-five paracetamols and washed them down with half a bottle of vodka. They'd found her just in time, but the baby had died. Vanessa came back at the beginning of year ten, smaller somehow and quieter than she'd ever been before. I found myself feeling sorry for her, but there was a part of me of me that had judged her. How could she have been so stupid? Not just stupid enough to go with a creep like Shane either, but to get pregnant!

What an idiot.

And now I was pregnant, only I was much older than Vanessa. Yet as the eldest of such a large family, I had seen so many babies brought into the house. I even remembered Sal vaguely, wrapped up in the blue shawl my Nan had made for my Dad when he was just a baby. I recalled the exhausted, elated expression on my mother's face each time, the proud puffed-up chest of my father. Each time he'd 'toast the little lady' and our house would be filled with his many associates, all of them dodgy, smelling of alcohol and cigarettes, leaning over the second-hand crib and congratulating him on producing yet another girl.

'When you gonna bring us a boy, Dan?' one of his mates Rory laughed when Hannah was born.

'I'm the only man of the house!' my father chuckled.

Sure enough, the twins were next, the last of the Carmichael girls. At that party, I had sat on the sofa and watched my father and his cronies sink more beer than we could afford, yet for once my mother wasn't wearing her sour expression. My father had come home from an absence that had lasted nearly six months and the majority of her pregnancy. I think then she had just been glad to have him back.

Not that it lasted long. Dad hadn't lived at home in years, appearing and disappearing at will: sending money when he could, falling silent when he couldn't. From time to time, he'd come to the house, his hands in his pockets like a teen, waiting for Mum to take him inside. Sometimes she'd make him a sandwich or a coffee; other times they'd disappear upstairs together for hours. Whatever the case, they were together – yet not together. The same as they'd always been, whether they actually lived in the same house or not.

'Dad's here!' Hannah would exclaim every time, beaming.

Each time Dad came back, Hannah was always sure he would stay. But could she really remember a time he had? I barely could.

'Don't get excited,' I'd warn her.

Sal would cut in cruelly, 'He's not staying, dimwit.'

And sure enough, Dad would give us all a hug, call us his princesses and then be on his way again. At the moment, he was living in as a kitchen porter at the Belle View Hotel on Roslin Road, just four streets away from where I was standing now. But I knew I would not go and see him and ask his advice. How could I? He had always been there, more or less, but he'd never truly been there for any of us.

A classic example: I'd been bullied at school. Mum had advised me to simply hit back, sure this would be the end of it. But she'd never met my bully, a bitch called Lorna. She was the type who never let up, so when I'd hit her back, she'd really gone to town on me. (Shona had just stood there, not moving, though I guess I should've been grateful she picked me back up off the floor. Thanks 'sis'!).

It was obvious I couldn't tell Mum Lorna had handed me my arse on a plate. So, I'd gone to see Dad at the house he'd lived at during that time, the one down near the seafront. A forty-year-old living in with some teen students from the local college was pretty weird, but it was all he could afford.

And the students loved him and his never-ending supply of weed, of course. He always had enough money for that shit.

I'd knocked on the door and a shirtless boy barely older than myself had answered, plumes of smoke billowing around him. Perhaps no other fresh air had hit the house in days. Behind the boy, I could see the muck of a house. It had not been cleaned in months: there were mouldy plates piled high in the sink, the carpet deep in rubbish and various other crap. My father practically fell out of the doorway, his stoned face lighting up at the sight of me.

'Lizzzzz…' he slurred after a short beat, as if he had to think first which of his girls I was. 'Come in!'

I just stood there. There was something so pathetic and sad about him, a grown man, standing next to the shirtless boy, surrounded by filth.

'I have to go.' I simply turned on my heel and walked back up the road.

He didn't call after me and it was never mentioned again. Perhaps my father did not even remember the encounter. Whatever, I knew I could not go to him now.

So, where?

Four

I looked at my watch. It had been roughly an hour and a half since Sal had left me at the bandstand. It was more than enough time to make it home on the bus and across the two fields to our house. Would she have spilled her guts to Mum?

I took my mobile from my pocket, half expecting a text from Mum, along with the curt words COME HOME NOW. Mum always wrote in capital letters, as if she didn't expect to be taken seriously otherwise. I visualised her, sitting at the long kitchen table, cigarette smouldering in the ashtray, giving her true feelings away. How many times had I stood before her like that, shame filling my boots, defiance rising in my chest?

She was a scary woman, my mother. Perhaps I would have been too had my children outnumbered me, six to one. Mum was a short woman, even shorter than me (and I was the shortest of all the Carmichael girls, or would be; even the twins were gaining on me at nearly eight years old). Sal and Amanda had taken after our father and Hannah was the tallest of all of us, nearly five ten at only thirteen, gangly and awkward, all arms and elbows.

Yet our mother was not just short, but tiny: her hands, her feet, her nose – everything about her was miniature. It was like an alien had come down from space and shrunk her with some kind of futuristic ray gun. She was painfully thin, no boobs to speak of, 'cus she liked cigarettes more than food. From a distance she could be mistaken for a skeletal child; it was only up close could you see the age in her eyes, the faded enthusiasm. A shock of frizzy hair stood out from her scalp, which from time to time she would attempt to dye, yet it would always go orange, no matter what the colour said on the box. Lines drew in her lips like a drawstring and she rarely wore make up, the grey pallor of her skin showing the world just how tired she was. And always, always, her catchphrase was the same in response to our protests at cleaning our rooms, helping out with the housework or whatever else we had been asked to do: 'Have I slipped into some kind of parallel dimension where I'm speaking Chinese? Do it!'

But regardless of her sometimes cold ways, she was a good mother. I had never doubted her first thought in the morning was us girls, or her last one at night. Despite her lack of money, Mum searched high and low all year round for the best inexpensive presents for birthdays and Christmas, without resorting to things that had fallen off the back of the lorry. On Christmas day, there was always a turkey on the table, sprouts and roasties and crackers. She was up every morning at the crack of dawn, preparing packed lunches. Dinner was always ready every evening, whether we wanted to eat it or not. There was no faddy eating in the Carmichael house: you got what you were given, and you ate it, or you were for one of Mum's other catchphrases, 'There are starving children in Africa, you know!'

'We're down, but not out,' she'd assert and us girls would mouth this behind her back and laugh and not really know what she meant.

When one of us came home crying from school, she'd let us cry in our rooms first before knocking tentatively on the door and asking what the problem was. If we didn't want to talk, Mum wouldn't make us. Instead, she would sit there on the end of the bed and wait. If we still didn't want to talk, she'd go back to the kitchen and make us a chocolate spread sandwich (usually only allowed at weekends). She'd deliver it to our rooms without a word, just a pat on the shoulder and that half-smile of hers.

I couldn't bear the thought of returning home, not yet. I couldn't stand before my mother and not only tell her I was pregnant, but that I wanted to get rid of it! Mum had been just nineteen years old when she had me; just a year older than I was now. She'd scrimped and saved and sacrificed for me and my sisters, with and without Dad's help over the years. She was the one true constant in my life. Without her, I would be nothing, quite literally. If I told her I wanted rid, surely it would be like me rejecting everything she had ever done for me?

I couldn't tell Mum I wanted an abortion.

Abortion. I'd been avoiding that word. 'Can't have this baby' and 'getting rid of the baby' were poor substitutes. Mrs Jenkin-No-S would have had me look up 'abortion' in a dictionary no doubt, like she did so many others.

'To truly know a word is to be able to define a word!' she would bark.

I scrabbled in my bag again and drew out my well-thumbed dictionary. A pang lanced through my chest as I read the message in the front from my mother: 'To Lizzie at Christmas, my little wordsmith', followed by a selection of kisses. I sighed and turned the pages through the As. There it was, *'Abort, verb: to terminate before completion; to cease development or die, ie. 'to abort a foetus'.'*

A foetus. A baby.

Oh God.

But I still had to find out more. Having the facts wouldn't make me less able to do what I needed to do. I didn't want to be 'the pregnant one'. I didn't want to bring up this baby all alone, with no money, no prospect of making any or stay in this town a moment longer than I had to. I wanted the future I was meant to have, not the one that was being rewritten for me right now by chance.

And that didn't make me a bad person.

Five

I walked towards the doctor's surgery. I'd made my decision. I just needed to find out how to implement it. I took a deep breath and pushed the door inwards…

'…Lizzie!'

There was a flash of royal blue and the smell of too much face powder. Mrs. Darby descended on me, pecking my cheek in that bird-like way of hers. Probably three hundred years old, Mrs. Darby always carried a voluminous shopping bag and an umbrella, even on the sunniest of days. She also lived across one of the two fields from my house. From time to time, Mrs. Darby would drop by unannounced and my mother would always entertain her, pouring tea for the Old Gossip and nodding, eyes glazed over.

'Ill, are you, dear?' Mrs Darby tutted, her expression teeming with fake sympathy. Really, the old bag wanted to know why I was there.

'Just picking up a prescription for Mum.' I said.

I was surprised at how the lie tripped off my tongue. Then my heart lurched: Mrs. Darby couldn't know the pharmacist in town collected them… could she? But then, there was very little Mrs. Darby didn't know, it seemed. Winby was a very small town and our own hamlet of Linwood beyond it, even smaller.

Yet the lie slipped by Mrs. Darby unnoticed. She patted my arm and said, 'Send her my love, won't you.'

With that, she waddled through the double doors of the surgery. I breathed a sigh of relief, then checked the rest of the waiting room. There was no one else there I knew, or more importantly, knew my mum. Phew.

I approached the counter. 'I need an appointment.'

'When?'

The bored-looking receptionist was barely out of her teens. I thought I recognised her from somewhere. Perhaps someone from college's sister? She wore too much make up, her hair scraped back in a vicious-looking ponytail. Three of her nails on her left hand were missing, revealing just gluey stubs underneath. The wonky clacking on the keyboard set my teeth on edge.

'Today?' My tone was hopeful.

The receptionist looked at me as if I was insane. 'We're booking for next week.'

I felt a surge of panic rise in my chest. 'I really need an appointment today?'

The receptionist went back to her screen and tapped a few buttons. Long enough to get my hopes up, until:

'Nah. We got nothing.'

I felt those familiar tears well up. 'Please.'

'Sorry.' Said the receptionist, clearly not sorry at all.

In a blur, I turned. As a door opened, I was faced with someone else I knew. It was just a girl from college, someone I only knew to say hello to in the corridor. She'd had Art with me and always sat at the back, texting.

'Lizzie.' She said, a big smile lighting up her face, 'I heard you got into the university you wanted? Well done.'

I couldn't remember the girl's name. I knew it began with 'L' – Laura, maybe?

'Thanks.' I stuttered. There was an awkward pause as we stood opposite each other, grasping for something to say. '… Did you?'

'No.' The girl shrugged. 'I don't think my portfolio was

good enough, didn't get in anywhere.'

'That's a shame.' I said, hardly able to believe these words were forming in my mouth. *I had more important things to deal with right now!*

'I'll try again next year.'

Optimism was painted across the girl's her face. I envied her for that. To her, anything seemed possible, when all I had and ever wanted was about to be snatched away from me.

'I have to go.'

As I began to turn, the girl caught my arm.

'Are you okay?' she said.

I wanted to say, 'Yes, fine,' and breeze away, so she – whoever she was – would never know. I didn't want to tell a stranger my business. I had barely exchanged twenty words with her in the past. She was just someone I saw and nodded at, no big deal.

Yet I was unable to look her in the eye or say anything without my lip quivering. Her eyes narrowed. She got it: she could see I was in trouble.

'Come for a coffee with me?' The girl said.

I found myself in a backstreet cafe with her, staring at dishwater brown coffee in a chipped mug, telling her everything that had happened that morning.

'Your sister sounds like a bitch.' The girl said.

'No, she's not.'

I was taken aback by my automatic defence of Sal. I probably would have merely agreed with the girl just twenty-four short hours ago. But then, my revision-obsessed sister had not dropped everything and come to me when I needed her. (Now, thanks to me, she probably never would again).

'Are you going to wait the week?' The girl enquired, '… For the doctor's appointment?'

'I guess I'll have to.'

I couldn't even … The thought made me feel like curling up and dying. How could I live with this for another seven days? Would I lose my nerve? Would I end up having this baby, simply by default?

'No, you don't have to.'

The girl set her bag on the tabletop and searched through it, drawing out her wallet. On it, her name, embroidered: NIKKI. I almost laughed. That wasn't even vaguely close to Laura. From her wallet, she drew out a bright pink business card and presented it to me.

'These guys will help you.' Nikki said.

'Thanks,' I accepted it, my eyes bright and wide.

She checked her watch. 'Go today. I'd come with you, except I have to …'

I smiled, catching sight of myself in the mirrored panel opposite. I looked more together than I felt. 'You've done enough. Thanks so much.'

Nikki gave my shoulder a little squeeze, then left, the bell on the café door tinkling as she disappeared through it. I turned the card over: on it, the name of a youth contraception service in a funky font. Cartoon eggs and sperm denoted it was serious, yet still 'for young people' in a pseudo-comforting manner.

My next stop.

Six

It took me a while to find the service Nikki had directed me to. It was a single door sandwiched between an arcade and a boarded-up ironmonger's on the seafront. There was no bright pink paint or funky font here: just a faded name on a buzzer, scrawled in biro. I could never have found it alone, I'd never even known it was there. I thanked Nikki again, this time in my head. I pressed the button and waited.

'Yes?' A high-pitched female voice trilled.

'I need to see someone.'

I prayed the voice would not ask the inevitable next question, 'What for?' Could I really reply, 'an abortion', down this buzzer??? To my relief, the buzzer sounded and the door unlocked for me.

I traipsed across the threshold. The hallway was every bit as filthy as that student house my father had lived in, all those years ago. The walls were marked and there were acres of post, leaflets and junk mail on the telephone table. A young woman with badly-dyed hair and wearing a hoodie and jeans appeared on the carpet-less stairs. She smiled in what she must have imagined was a reassuring manner.

'Hi, I'm Helen.' She said, 'come on up.'

We ascended the rickety, creaking stairs towards a small white door with a leaded window at the top. Helen opened it and ushered me inside. I was expecting another filthy, depressing room with scarred white walls. Instead, I was faced with leather sofas, a coffee machine, fluffy rugs. The walls were a light pink and there were posters in glass frames, all on the subject of contraception: SAFE SEX IS SMART SEX was emblazoned on one (a little too late for me).

'So, what can I do for you...?' Helen settled down in one of the chairs, bidding me to do the same.

'My name's Elizabeth.' My mouth was sour and dry.

'Elizabeth.' Helen noted my name down on a clipboard. She waited, that uber-fake 'don't-worry-everything-will-be-fine' smile etched on her face.

'I'm pregnant.' Before she could say anything (or maybe before I could change my mind?) I quickly followed up with, 'Iwantanabortion.'

Saying the words aloud for the first time, I felt myself wince. I half-expected her to, as well. Helen's face betrayed nothing: she simply noted something down on that clipboard.

'I see,' she said. 'Have you discussed this with your boyfriend?'

I could see Mike's face in my mind's eye. The blank expression that always maddened me. His never-ending well of self-belief that he was right and everyone else was wrong (especially me). I could hear the tremulous teenage defiance in his voice that always made me cringe when he argued with his father. He was not old enough to take this on board, despite the fact he was older than me. I knew that.

'Yes.' I lied.

'And what about your family, Elizabeth?' Helen continued.

Mute, I nodded. I had told Sal, hadn't I? That much was true at least. My stomach turned itself in knots, I hated all these lies. But it was the only way.

Half an hour later and I had a yet another pink card in my hand, an appointment for the next day at the general hospital noted on it. I stared at it on the bus all the way home.

Helen had explained all the options to me. There were two kinds of abortion, medical and surgical. The former was for early pregnancy like mine and involved taking just two pills, a bit like the morning after pill. The baby would be flushed out: gone, just like that.

It seemed so easy. Too easy?

I skulked into the house just before dinner. I was sure Sal must have told Mum by now. Yet everyone was grouped around the table, chatting and laughing. I hovered on the outside of it all, watching the rest of them. Their lives hadn't changed but gone on uninterrupted. Nice for some.

Mum heaped spaghetti and sauce on my plate and pushed it in front of me. 'Good day?'

I knew what she really meant: 'Where have you been?' But I just smiled and told her I was at Shona's. Sal met my gaze across the table; there was that sneer again on her top lip: *Liar.* But I averted my gaze from my sister's and twirled spaghetti around my fork.

It would all be over, soon.

Seven

The next morning, I kissed my mother goodbye. I had everything I needed packed inside my college bag: a few toiletries, a toothbrush, even a nightie, even though Helen had told me I would be a day case at the hospital. I'd perched a few books on the top of it all, just in case Mum thought to look inside. She never had before, but I felt sure her X-Ray eyes could see directly into my heart and find out what I was about to do that day.

But Mum barely looked up from her morning cup of tea and first cigarette. She just smiled and said, 'See you tomorrow.'

I'd told them all I was going to Shona's for the night, which in part was true: I would be going to hers after I had gone to the hospital. I couldn't face going straight home after the abortion; my face would give me away for sure. I'd already called and arranged my alibi with a dubious Shona the night before.

'If they call for any reason during the day, tell them I'm in the shower or something.' I'd said to my best friend, 'Then let me know and if I can, I'll call them back from my mobile.'

Shona didn't sound happy. 'So, what are you really doing?'

'I'll tell you tomorrow night.'

In truth, I wasn't too sure what I was doing. Though Helen had gone to great pains to explain what would happen, her words had seemed impossibly far away. I had seen only her lips moving. I'd played the game, looking at the posters and the leaflets she had shown me; I'd nodded where I was supposed to and repeated what she had asked me to. In reality, I had been on autopilot. Just one thing had been going through my mind the whole time.

I want this over.

Now, in a few short hours, it would be. The general hospital was not in town, but the best part of twenty miles away in Exmorton, the bigger of the two towns on our side of the headland. Helen had advised me 'the procedure' (she'd called it that throughout our entire meeting) was not available in Winby's small cottage hospital. I took my place on a coach, amongst a variety of old people going on day trips. As the vehicle flashed by fields and woodland, I realised how isolated from the rest of civilisation we were. Real life started so many miles away: proper healthcare, university, even careers. It didn't seem right, somehow.

Walking into the large general hospital felt bewildering and scary. The place was like a labyrinth. I ended up in Urology (I didn't even know what that was), before being directed by a sympathetic porter with a kindly face to the right ward. I wondered if he would be so kindly if he knew what I was about to do.

Arriving at reception, a young nurse with purple hair and Doc Marten's took me to a ward full of sad-looking girls. Some of them had their mothers with them; others had their boyfriends; a couple of them had both. Only I was alone.

'Is there anyone I can call for you?' The nurse said.

I shook my head. I yanked the curtain around my bed shut, so I could see no one else and no one else could see me. A terrible sense of trepidation gripped me: was I doing the right thing? I knew in my heart I was. Yet why didn't it feel like it?

The rest of the day passed in a blur. A doctor came and examined me, felt my tummy and muttered something about gestation to an eager-looking medical student. A psychiatrist who pretended she wasn't a psychiatrist stopped by for a chat: 'How do I feel?' *Terrible,* I wanted to say, but bravado would not allow me to. I simply nodded, my default setting of the past few days.

Then... nothing. I could hear the voices of other patients and somewhere a girl was crying, her mother offering soothing words. I felt strangely empty, like I wasn't really there, like this was all just a bad dream.

What felt like years passed and a Filipino nurse arrived with a small cup with a single pill inside. Squat, no-nonsense, she offered it to me with no judgement on her face, yet my shame insisted it must still be there. Would this be what it would be like forever, now? I hesitated, my hand over the cup.

'Are you sure, darling?' The Filipino nurse said, her words melting together in her thick accent.

I looked up at her at last and I saw only sympathy in her eyes.

'Yes.' I said finally – and took the pill, washing it down with water.

I hadn't really thought about what would happen next. I suppose I had imagined the baby would simply disappear, despite Helen's careful and vivid explanations. Knowing what would happen and knowing it *for real* though were two very different things. A second pill later – the full course – and I felt the familiar gripes of period-like pain and panic fluttered my heart a little.

No turning back now.

I felt heat envelop me, then nausea. The pain grew in intensity. A trip to the toilet later confirmed the pregnancy was ending: blood. I remembered one of the leaflets I had read: the passing of the 'egg sac' would be next – *don't look, don't look*. Egg sac. They meant the baby, of course. 'Just think of it as a collection of cells', the psychiatrist had said. But wasn't that what all of us were?

My hand hovered over the toilet handle, then I pulled it.

Eight

'You alright, darling?' The Filipino nurse said as I gathered my things together. 'I call someone for you?'

Tight-lipped, I murmured a barely audible 'no thanks'. Shona had arranged for her father – home for once – to come and pick me up. They waited in the car park, Shona's curious face pressed against the glass of the car window.

'You look like shit.' She declared as I clambered ginger-ly into the back seat.

'Shona.' Her father scolded.

Shona merely pulled a face at him, not caring he could see her doing so. I wondered where she got the nerve to do that.

'Everything okay, Elizabeth?' He said.

'Just visiting.'

This seemed to satisfy him. Shona gave me a look in re-turn that told me she didn't believe me for one second. Later that night, she listened wide-eyed as I told her the full story.

'Do you regret it?' she demanded.

I thought of the 'procedure' as Helen called it. It had been much harder than I had expected. But then I thought of Mike and Mum: how I would never have to have those awk-ward conversations or have to justify myself to Mike's dad or my sisters, barring Sal. I'd already planned to tell her it had been a false alarm, anyway. No one need ever know for real, not ever. It could be swept under the carpet, consigned to a terrible moment in time; dealt with and forgotten.

Even so, something told me I would never truly forget. Though I didn't regret my decision – I'd had too much to lose – I felt a well of sadness growing within me. I had not entered into the abortion lightly. I had felt I had had no choice, if I were to have the future I was meant to have. I deserved that future. I had worked hard - too hard! - to have it snatched from me at the very last moment.

'No.' I said. And meant it.

The weeks that followed passed in a blur: my exam results arrived. I had done as well as my course tutors had predicted. My eighteenth birthday was a small affair, just family, followed by combined 'goodbye' drinks with friends and associates, as our friendship group all prepared for our new lives. There was packing for university, plus the organisation of overdrafts, bills, and other 'adult' stuff, not to mention the excitement and trepidation of what was to come. I focused on university and glossed over what had happened. Even looking at Sal's accusatory face over the breakfast table could not get me down. Though I had told her about the supposed 'false alarm', I sensed she did not believe me. But rather than tell the truth or discuss the situation with my confused and angry fifteen-year-old sister, I chose to ignore her.

But there was one person I could not ignore: Mike. Every time I saw him, it was like all my nerve endings shrieked, *tell him what you did*. But what would that achieve? He would never have wanted the child and even if he had, I didn't anyway. Better still that he never knew the sadness of having to make the decision.

That's how I justified it to myself, anyway. I knew I had been wrong not to involve him. Guilt kept me away from him in those final few weeks before university. We were going to different ones anyway, several hundred miles apart. I told myself it would never have worked beyond Christmas, anyway.

So, I watched his confusion, then his anger as I barely paid him any attention on nights out; or when I 'forgot' to return his calls. Voicemails and text messages arrived, demanding to know why I was treating him this way. Finally, a last text arrived with a single word: *BITCH.*

And then, silence. It was over. I absorbed the empty, hollow victory and continued with my winding my life at home up. I would be out of there before I knew it: life – my real life - could finally begin.

But there was one person I'd forgotten.

Nine

Mike's disappearance from my life in the last few weeks before university did not go unnoticed by Mum. She made veiled queries about the split, but I batted them away. I had never been able to lie to her anyway and especially not this time, for fear of unravelling the truth about the abortion.

A day before leaving for university, Mum came into my room as I was doing the last of my packing.

'I saw Philip in town.' Mum said. Philip was Shona's dad's name. I didn't look up, for fear of Mum's gaze burning a hole in my heart and exposing me. 'He says he hopes you feel better?'

I tried to bluff my way through it. 'I'm fine.'

'He says he picked you up from the hospital.' Mum's voice deliberately calm. I could tell she was trying her hardest to keep hold of herself. So Philip had not believed I was visiting someone after all.

I still persisted: 'I told him, I was visiting someone.'

'Who?'

The few weeks that had passed had made me complacent. I couldn't think of a name on the spot. 'Just—just a girl from college.' I stammered.

'Who?' Mum demanded.

'Just a girl! You don't know her!' I shrieked, desperate to get out of the conversation. I was not going to do this. Not now, not a single day before I left for university.

Then, Mum's bull's eye: 'He says he picked you up from the left side.'

The left side … What people in town called the side of the hospital that covered maternity, obstetrics, gynaecology. How many times had Dad careered the car around that massive car park, negotiating the stupid one-way system, as my mum puffed and panted in labour? *She knew.*

So I told her.

There were tears, but not for the reasons I expected. I had thought Mum would plead the case for her lost grandchild; or that she could point the finger at me, saying I was judging her and our lives by not wanting to be the same as her.

Instead, it wasn't just Mike I should have felt guilt over. I had not allowed my mother to support me in my decision, either. I tried to justify myself, make her see I had never meant her harm, but somehow that was worse. I had barely considered her feelings or needs as a mother at all. I had decided, without asking, what Mum's reaction would be: *that* was what she was upset about. She had wanted to be there for me, support me, in whatever decision I had chosen.

I had not allowed her.

The evening ended in a kind of limbo state. I went to bed on my very last night at home with a head full of thoughts and a heart full of regrets. Not because of the abortion, but because of the way I had handled it.

I thought back to the mothers and the boyfriends on my ward. All those other girls and women had had their loved ones for support. It hadn't been just for them either, it was for those mothers and boyfriends too. I recalled the crying girl and the sound of her mother's soothing voice, comforting her daughter, but also herself: *at least she was there, a part of her daughter's life when she needed her most.* What did my mum have, now? I wondered if we could ever find our way back.

In the morning Mum presented bacon and eggs in honour of me leaving – usually it was just cereal and toast. My sisters gave me small going-away presents: a writing set from Amanda; gel pens from Sal; a random sparkly unicorn figurine from Hannah, typical of her.

The twins had drawn me a picture of the house, with a giant portrait of me standing over it with a big red smile on my face and green hair. Dad arrived with helium balloons that wouldn't fit in Mum's tiny car with the luggage, so we set them off from the garden with our names and address attached to them.

'I wonder who will write back!' Hannah enthused.

I envied her. Everything was always so positive for her, yet even on the eve of an exciting new life, I felt only fear. *Typical me.*

Then the time came when I had to get in the car with Mum to drive to the station. Dad and the girls waved for as long as the car took to get to the end of the country lane. As silence descended between me and Mum, I wanted to say 'sorry' but I had said it a thousand times the night before. What did 'sorry' mean, really? We drove the hour it took to the station, without saying a word, just the occasional sorrowful glance from Mum at me in the rear-view mirror.

At the rural station in the middle of nowhere, students shoved their cases and bags onto a state-of-the-art train that seemed to have no place amongst the greenery. Irritated businessmen and women, not used to sharing the narrow platform, tutted and shook out newspapers in an attempt to gain more arm-space.

I looked at the train and felt as if everything was going to change. I would go and never come back quite the same again. Perhaps that wouldn't even be one of my many flights of fancy, but the truth.

'Elizabeth?' I looked back at Mum, startled; she never called me by my full name. 'This is for you.'

She handed me a small trinket box. I accepted it without a word. I felt as if I didn't deserve it after the way I had treated her, but I knew she would be offended if I refused it. Inside, was a silver ring with a green stone, my favourite colour.

'I got it on the market.' Mum gabbled. 'I hope it fits…?'

I slipped it on my finger. It did.

'Thank you.' I gulped, barely able to look her in the eye.

Suddenly Mum enveloped me in her bony embrace.

'I'm so proud of you, you know.'

And at that moment I felt my heart would burst. She still loved me after all. We would be okay.

The guard's whistle went. Mum urged, 'go, go'. I jumped onto the train and waved from a window. My impossibly tiny mother got tinier as she faded into the distance. A new life could begin.

As I sat back in my chair in the crowded train, I could hear a phone ringing no one was answering. Then, a little embarrassed as I clocked the exasperated expressions of other travellers, I realised it was my own.

I dug the phone out of my pocket – and on the screen was MUM. A little confused, I pressed the ACCEPT button.

'Hello?' I said …

Mum

*'We never know the love of a parent until we
become parents ourselves.'*
Henry Ward Beecher

Ten

I was back in those grotty toilets at the marketplace. The phone to my ear. I blinked, my world out of focus. The light hurt my eyes.

'Lizzie? Lizzie… are you there?'

On the other end of the line, Mum sounded far away, as if she were underwater. For a second, I felt like I was not even there, but flying above myself, as if I was listening out for someone else speaking instead.

'I-I'm here.' I stammered, though my voice felt and sounded impossibly low somehow. 'Must be a bad reception?'

My confusion lessened. The world around me swam into focus: I was outside the toilet cubicles, looking at my reflection in the aluminium mirror. I looked down at my left hand: from it, the positive pregnancy tester dangled. *Of course.*

Nausea hit me. I leaned against the sinks, willing Mum to get off the line. The lemming in me wanted to yell, simply, 'I'm pregnant!' down the phone at her. Even I knew that would not go down well.

'Is Sal with you?' Mum said, 'I just went to her room and she's not there. She didn't tell me she was going out.'

Sal … Something niggled at me, though I wasn't sure why. 'She's not with me.' I replied. *Get off the phone!*

'Lizzie, this is serious. I'm worried.'

I sighed but did my best to repress it. I had bigger things

to worry about, but Mum didn't know that. I grabbed my bag, pushed the door out to the marketplace. The noise came in deafeningly as stallholders and customers jostled for attention and a bargain, making me raise my voice.

'I can't see her in the marketplace.'

I elbowed my way through the crowd and the stalls, though the noise swallowed up my voice and my mother's reply. There was the butcher's. The fishmonger's. The old lady with a trestle table full of junk. Same old, same old. But...

... I stopped in front of another stall: an elderly man stood there in overalls, pot plants and seedling trays for sale. The old man gave me a hopeful, gummy smile, but I wasn't buying. For some reason, I could sense something had changed here, but I wasn't sure what or how.

Must be my imagination.

'Lizzie?' Mum's voice pierced the disorder at last. 'Can you see her?'

'No.' I said at last, 'Sorry, Mum.'

A fatal mistake. I never apologised to Mum, ever. It had always been a little power struggle between us. I had noticed, aged eight or nine, that Mum didn't always get things right. Yet whenever *she* made mistakes, she didn't seem to feel the need to apologise. I had decided there and then I wouldn't either. Over the years, the saltiness between us could have powered both the Pacific and Atlantic oceans.

'What's the matter?' Suspicion tinged every single one of Mum's words.

'Nothing.' I cursed my moment of weakness. Mum had almost supernatural powers anyway, without giving her the green light something was wrong!

'Hmmmmmm,' Mum said in that way of hers that means, *'I don't believe a word you say, Missy.'*

On the other end of the line, I heard the front door slam.

'... Sal!' Mum was still on the phone, forgetting she was

shouting right in my ear: 'Where the hell have you been???'

Back at home, Sal muttered something. But Mum wasn't listening.

'Well, stay here and watch the twins, will you?' She said to Sal, then her attention was back on me. 'I'm coming to get you, Lizzie.'

'No, there's no need … I'm just tired.'

'Don't lie to me, Lizzie!'

There was no way of getting out of this one, I realised. And did I want to? As harsh as Mum's reaction might be, I needed someone's help … And she was my mother, after all.

'Fine.' I said, still resenting her bulldozer ways. 'I'll come home on the bus right now.'

'You do that.' Mum rang off.

A sense of dread settled over me like mist as I made for the bus. As the vehicle rattled and rolled through the country lanes, I told Mum my news a million times in my head. What was best: 'I'm pregnant' or 'I'm having a baby'? Which was the least likely to antagonise her? I pictured her saying a thousand different words, but all of them were negative: *Why were Mike and I not careful? How could we be so stupid? What were we going to do???*

As the bus stopped in the square by the old closed down pub, I groaned: Mum had sent Amanda to meet me. My sister sat in the broken bus shelter, smoking one of her not-so-secret cigarettes. Dressed in her uniform of pink tracksuit, denim jacket and white high tops, Amanda's make-up was perfect, not a blonde hair out of place. My sister seemed to believe even in the middle of nowhere a model scout could spot her. Later she'd film herself on her phone for her stupid YouTube channel, pouting and flipping her hair, yet another Kim K wannabe.

'What've you done?' Amanda dropped her stub and popping some gum in her mouth as I got off the bus.

'None of your business.' I retorted.

Amanda smiled and offered me the gum packet. 'Mum will tell me, anyway.'

We walked in silence across the fields. As our house at the bottom of the valley appeared in view, I felt my heart sink even further in my chest. Perhaps it had been a mistake not to allow my mother to come and fetch me? We could have gone to a café or something. There, she would have been forced to listen, because there was one thing Mum hated more than anything else: a scene in public. Always, it was 'Don't cause a scene' or, 'Don't you dare, people are looking!'

Obviously, all of us had enacted a small revenge on Mum at some point in public: eight-year-old Amanda had sung an expletive-ridden rap song Christmas-carol style, in perfect soprano, whilst bored at a school play. A four-year-Sal had screamed, 'She's trying to kill me!' as Mum dragged her out of a toy shop. Even do-gooding Hannah had yelled as an under-five, 'Look Mummy, look! A really fat lady!' as a morbidly obese woman had attempted to board the bus we were all on once. Throughout all of these 'shenanigans' (Mum's word, not mine), I had seen my mother's drawstring mouth become even tighter, her face ageing ten years in a single moment.

I could have had a sensible, adult discussion with Mum on neutral ground with her as my captive audience. But home was Mum's domain. Worse still, I had left her stewing there for forty minutes over what I could possibly be hiding. I was an idiot!

No music was playing as I walked through the front door. That was another bad sign. Mum told me once she only ever turned the radio off when she had 'too many thoughts rolling around in her head'. There was also cigarette smoke; lots of it. Mum usually made some attempt to smoke outside, hovering on the doorstep of the open back door to the patio, even first thing in the morning or in the middle of winter. But not today. The back door was closed. A gross, smoky fug enveloped the room, making my nostrils twitch. Mum was seated in what we girls called her 'interrogation mode': at the table, two packets of Marlboro Red and a lighter at her elbow, countless butts overflowing in the ashtray.

'Go to your room, Amanda.' Mum, who was barely looking at her, fixed her gaze on me. *Oh God, this was not good.*

Amanda shrugged and did as she was told, shooting me a 'Good luck!' expression on her way past. Sal, Hannah and the twins would already be in theirs, straining to hear the battle beyond through the cottage's ultra-thick old walls.

Mum pushed a chair out from under the table with her foot and indicated for me to take it. 'Sit down.'

It was not an option to refuse. I could sense the fury in Mum just waiting to unleash itself and, in that moment, I really hated her. Had I not been good enough over my near-eighteen years to be given the benefit of the doubt? Had I really been that difficult a daughter? *Screw you, Mum.*

Before she could proper start on me: 'I'm pregnant.'

I had expected an immediate eruption from Mum. What I got was more like someone had letting the air out of her. She seemed to deflate, like a beach ball. Whatever Mum had been thinking during the time it had taken me to get home, it was clear she had not been expecting this.

She opened her mouth, then closed it. She took a cigarette out of its packet but did not light it. The one thing she hated more than the idea of us girls smoking, was smoking whilst or around pregnant women. The only times fresh air circulated our house, unbidden, was when Mum was pregnant. Literally the moment she gave birth however, she was out on the hospital steps having a crafty fag before Dad could stop her.

'And Mike's the father?'

'Of course he is,' I snapped.

'Don't take that tone with me, lady!' An uncomfortable silence. Mum turned the unlit cigarette around in her fingers, over and over. '… When?'

'What?' But I knew what she meant. When had this happened, how pregnant was I? I sighed, 'I don't know … Two, two and a half weeks ago?'

'Okay.' Mum said, which I thought was strange. How could this be okay? But I said nothing, waiting for her to go on. Mum flicked her Zippo a couple of times and then continued.

'… Okay. We can figure this out.'

My heart leapt in my chest at last. She was going to help me. But what did that mean? Even I was unsure what I wanted to do.

'Does Mike know?'

'No.'

'Do you want him involved?' Mum demanded.

I hesitated. A weird part of me never wanted to see Mike again, just because it would be simpler that way. Mike had been my boyfriend less than a year, but we were hardly love match of the century. Our relationship was strictly social, no great meeting of minds. Something inside me told me my pregnancy should not keep us together or bind us in time, whatever the outcome. Yet somehow, it just seemed wrong to exclude him.

'Yes.' I said finally.

'Okay.' Mum said again, as if getting various things straight in her own head, her gaze off in the distance. 'Well, I can call the university for you.'

I didn't understand what she meant at first. Then it dawned on me: Mum was assuming I would have the baby and stay at home. But did I want to? I thought of the other solution: abortion. Just the word made me shudder. I wasn't sure if I could do it. I could feel university falling from my reach, but a small part of me didn't seem to care. I was surprised: it had been everything to me as little as a few short hours ago. Yet despite this realisation, a part of me burned with a secret anger at Mum for having made the decision, rather than actually asking me.

'What if I don't want the baby?' I said coldly.

Mum stopped flicking the Zippo lid, looked me right in the eye. 'Don't you?'

I hesitated. Was I really going to tell my mother I wanted a termination, out of sheer saltiness? It seemed foolish, especially when my gut instinct was telling me to hang fire. Ironically, another of my mother's many catchphrases came back to haunt me right that at that moment, 'when in doubt, do without.' But what did that mean: do without making the decision to have an abortion? Or do without the baby? I was confused.

'I don't know.' I admitted.

Mum's expression seemed to soften at last and she abandoned the lighter, reaching out across the table, squeezing my hand in her bony one. 'I know, darling. It's scary. I remember it well.' She said quietly.

Of course. Mum had not been much older than I was now when she had me. If anyone knew how to get me through this, Mum did. Though I had always strived to be independent since infancy, rejecting my mother's warnings and comfort throughout my childhood, I needed her to show me the way now.

Didn't I?

Eleven

'It's all logistics,' Mum had said, 'If you get it right, you can have everything you always wanted, including a little baby. It's a win-win.'

I'd been dubious. 'But university…?'

I could see my new, adult life getting further and further away … If I didn't make some attempt to snatch it back, wouldn't I regret it? Mum had always told us, 'If you have no money, education is your only hope.' All of us had worked hard at school (okay, all of us except Amanda!), but the rest of us had taken Mum at her word … And now she was telling me I should wait? It didn't make sense.

'Just wait a bit,' Mum said, 'There's no reason you can't go when the baby starts school.'

'But that's five years away nearly!' I wailed, a sudden panic washing over me. I felt paralysed. I knew, somehow, I wanted to keep the baby, yet I felt terrified at the prospect of being in limbo while I waited for it to grow up. Could I really wait that long? I felt sure I would wither away and die in the meantime.

'Darling,' Mum said with a smile, 'those five years will fly by.'

She'd seemed so sure. I found myself telling my sisters my news not even an hour later. As I had predicted, Sal curled her upper lip at me, before returning to her room. But I needn't have worried about Amanda, who shrugged and said, 'You got any cravings yet, then?'

Hannah had whooped, 'I'm going to be an Aunty!' and flung her arms around me. The twins piled on top of us too, laughing and for a moment, I forgot my own fears and let myself be swept along with it.

A baby in the house. It couldn't be so bad, could it? Perhaps it really was as simple as Mum said: *so, what if most people went to university, then had a career, then a baby …* I was intelligent, I was hard working. I could bump baby to the top of the list and have the other two later.

Of course, Dad needed to be told. Mum called him over and he turned up all smiles. Knowing him too well, Mum broke the news herself. I was consigned to the bedroom I shared with Amanda. We listened as best we could as we heard my father's raised voice. Then we heard a chair go over, just about catching *'This is your fault…'* not to mention my mother's sweary, incredulous reply. I could just imagine the hurricane downstairs, the bitterness my mother saved just for my Dad: irresponsible. *Loser. Weak.*

About an hour into the ruckus, Hannah and the twins appeared, all sniffles, trying to be brave. Amanda fetched out her box of treats. She worked a few hours a week in a nail salon as part of her beauty course and like all us Carmichael girls, she had a sweet tooth. She'd take the remaining wages she didn't spend on beauty products to the penny sweet shop in the arcade, saving them all from prying eyes and fingers in a red and white spotted box under the bed. Because she shared a room with me, it had a little padlock on it and the key hung around a chain on her wrist.

'Can't be too careful, greedy cows in this house grazin'.' She'd say.

But today she shared with all of us and it was only Sal who wasn't present. She'd stopped by at the landing when she'd heard us talking, but when offered the treasured red and white spotted box, Sal had just turned up her nose. She walked out, muttering something about us all getting diabetes.

'Bitch.' Amanda had called after her, but I'd felt sorry for Sal at that moment. She just wasn't able to let her guard down, ever; not even with her own family.

A couple of hours later and my name was called from downstairs by my mother. I appeared at the top of the stairs, hesitant, expecting to see my father's angry face peering up. He wasn't there though, so I crept down, towards the living room. Both my parents stood in the middle of the room. My father's face was flushed red, my mother's hair practically standing on end from the stress of the argument. But both were making an attempt to dampen down their real feelings and control their fury with each other, just for me, just for that moment.

'Your father has something to say to you.' My mother said pointedly.

I looked to Dad, expectant. After hearing the commotion downstairs, I wasn't sure I could believe he would not go off on one at me. He looked as if he wanted to. But perhaps my mother had shamed him into it, for the many moments of our lives he had missed (or perhaps he had finally realised himself), because instead he simply told me it would all be okay. We hugged, and I let myself believe his and Mum's words. They were on my side. Everything would be okay now.

Phone calls were made, and it wasn't long before Mike and his father, Francis were seated awkwardly in our front room. Francis was an elderly man, too old to have kept the interest of his much younger wife. Mike's mother Maria had left home when Mike was just five years old, arriving from time to time to pick him up and spirit him away to a succession of uncles' homes. A few weeks here, a few months there, but she would always drop him off again with Francis. The excuse was always same, 'I just need to sort myself out' and Maria would be all kisses and cuddles, promising her little boy she would return for him.

When Mike was ten Maria came back after a particularly long absence, this time with a new brother for him: James. Far from solidifying the family unit as she had hoped – she was married now, she told Mike on a trip to MacDonald's – Mike out-and-out rejected her and James and whoever the new husband was, telling her he never wanted to see any of them again. He actually did (Francis was far too old-school to allow his son to live in the same town as his mother and not see her), but Mike never lived with Maria again, nor James or his stepfather.

A part of me had wanted to cry when Mike had told me that story. It had been a rare moment of intimacy for him. Usually Mike had his guard up like Sal; sure people were coming in at him from either side, just itching to have a go. The hurt on his features was so tangible, he had looked like a little boy in that moment, despite the lip ring and the tattoo on his neck that had nearly given his father a heart attack. I had hated his mother in those moments, but also Mike's father for allowing it to continue. Mike had needed some-one to step in for him, fight his corner, yet Francis had al-lowed a ten-year-old boy to make that huge decision! Mike said he tortured himself over it, every day. Should he have forgiven his mother? Was choosing Francis the right thing? Had he been wrong in not getting to know his own brother? Mike's life had meant fleeting moments of James' birthday parties; snatched dinners after school; the odd weekend out-ing. During these times, the stepfather would affect his jolly laugh and Maria would look adoringly at both her boys, yet Mike would always feel sure she must love James more and he was the outsider.

It was unsurprising then that Mike stalked his way through life, his shoulders hunched, his fists clenched. He was unable to believe anyone could offer anything for its own sake, without an ulterior motive. Though he had let me into his life, I was someone to hang out with, not a real person in my own right; I knew that. Sometimes I caught him looking at me, as if he couldn't believe I was with him and he was the luckiest boy in the world. But most of the time he reserved the same lack of regard for me as one would a toothbrush, mug or flannel. Handy to have, but ultimately disposable.

Now he had been summoned to my parents' home, with his father, for the ultimate awkward situation in any young lad's life: *what were his intentions towards me and the baby I was carrying?*

I saw anger and humiliation in Mike's eyes and most of it was directed at me. *You stupid bitch*, his eyes said.

Hurt and confusion blossomed inside me. I could not have done this on my own, I could accept only half of the blame. I had not forced him to drink all those beers, nor chase them with whiskey with Ben and the rest of his cronies in The Moon those few short weeks ago. I had been there as Mike threw up in the pub toilets. I'd stood by and watched and not interfered as Mike had attempted to win the money back he'd lost in the earlier pool game to Ben's mate Drew.

Drew was a new guy we hadn't seen before, who was keen on confrontation and spent the whole night baiting Mike. Mike couldn't back down, throwing good money after bad, the argument brewing throughout, ready to erupt and end the night. I had sunk vodka after vodka waiting for Mike, then run after him when the fight had broken out that had him ejected from the premises, even though I had secretly thought the whole argument was Mike's fault and that he should have walked away. I had been the good girlfriend! Later, I had made him feel better like good girlfriends do, forgetting only the condoms in his wallet pocket and the notion of 'safe sex', in my own drunken state. But then, so had he.

Despite the unspoken blame game between us, the real grown-ups droned on about responsibility and plans and contingency measures. Old and pale, Francis looked impossibly frail, his skin and white hair turned yellow with nicotine like the pages of an old book. I knew Francis could only be in his early seventies – Mike had mentioned it once – which made him barely older than my own grandfather on my mother's side, whom the twins still called GanGan.

GanGan was seventy-one years old and strong like a gnarled old tree, in comparison to Francis who looked as if a puff of wind would blow him over. GanGan had lived a life on the move with the army, then as a landscape gardener. He chased after work and like my own father, turned up randomly, sometimes staying a few days, other times a few months. My grandmother had died from breast cancer when my mother was just twelve. When I was a child, my mother's two older sisters Grace and Rebecca had followed from the same disease, taken too soon. GanGan and my mother were the last of their kind and wasn't difficult to see why my mother had chosen a man like my father. He was the only type of man she had ever known.

So, if Francis was too old to have kept Mike's mother's interest, he was far too old to have a son as young as Mike. Listening to the old man, my heart lurched. Word after word, his out-of-date ideas and concepts poured out of him: we needed to think about what others would say. I should be kept in the house for my 'confinement' (WTH?). After the birth, Mike and I should get married.

'I don't think anyone's getting married,' my mother cut in, with cold authority. Then her eyes darted to me and then resentfully, towards Mike, 'Unless of course the kids want to?'

Kids. So typical of her to describe us like that, I thought. Though she did have a point: I didn't feel old enough to get married. But then I didn't exactly feel old enough to have a baby, either. Even so, I found myself shaking my head enthusiastically: *no, I did not want to get married.* I saw Mike was making the same gesture and felt relieved.

The meeting came to an abrupt, business-like conclusion about an hour later, with my father and Francis shaking hands whilst my mother, Mike and I watched incredulously. It was decided: Mike would continue with university as planned and complete his first year. I would stay at home with my parents and have the baby. Mike would visit where possible. The following summer, we would look at our options again. I had hoped to be able to speak to Mike on my own – this was our business after all, no one else's! - but Francis spirited him away in his little Metro.

I followed them out to the car like a lost sheep. 'Call me…?'

Mike shrugged and said simply, 'Yeah.'

'Thank God that's over.' Mum poured herself a large gin, even though it was barely five in the evening.

'Funny bloke, that Francis.' My father mused.

'You'd think he'd never met a child born 'out of wedlock' before.' Mum said, actually doing the inverted commas with her fingers. So embarrassing.

My parents were not married, either. My mother wore a ring on her engagement finger: the only thing my Dad had ever given her besides us girls, she'd say when she had had one too many. Mum always answered to 'Carmichael' too, even though technically her surname was Dale, the same as GanGan's.

There were no wedding photographs of my parents when they were young, standing on church or register office steps, their faces hopeful for the future. There were no celebrations of milestones achieved in the relationship. I wondered now if history was repeating itself and I was destined to have the same kind of relationship my parents had with

Mike for the next twenty years: together and yet not?

I shuddered at the thought. Already I wondered if I had done the right thing: not in keeping the baby, but in keeping Mike. I guessed only time would tell.

Twelve

My mother stood over me as I logged in the university computer system and withdrew from my place. With a click of the mouse, I was out of the running. A few days later, they wrote to me: did I want to defer my place? I had no idea. Perhaps I wouldn't even want to do that course anymore once the baby got here? Maybe I would want to do something else. Or perhaps I wouldn't even want to go to university! Mum's words came back to me a second time, 'When in doubt, do without.' With a heavy heart, I ticked 'no' on the reply slip and returned it in the enclosed stamped addressed envelope.

Just three weeks after news of my pregnancy broke, there had been only two more fleeting meetings between Mike and I, before he needed to leave for university. We tried to be as 'normal' as possible, pretending our thoughts in that initial meeting had never happened. Then we were at the train station, saying goodbye. Things were strained between us and I wondered if it was the moment I would look back on as losing him forever, even though he handed me a card with I LOVE YOU printed on the front. Inside was scrawled, 'Forever, Mike x', but I couldn't believe the spidery handwriting any more than my own heart. Could he? I wondered how long we would limp on, then pushed the unwanted thought to the bottom of my brain and concentrated on the positives instead. We could make it. We had to. There was a baby to think about. Besides, who else would have me?

Before long I was throwing up every day between the hours of seven and eight in the morning, causing my sisters to whinge I was hogging the bathroom. Even Hannah and the twins' initial enthusiasm was soon forgotten as they found the toilet occupied at the exact time they needed to use it before going to school. Mum held my hair back and batted their complaints away. She even took to waking them early, but even that didn't diffuse the situation, for Hannah in particular was not a morning person. She would sit at the kitchen table in pyjamas, legs crossed, a face like thunder, eating dry cornflakes out the box and sulking. True to form, Sal was amused by the state I found myself in, smiling and tutting in mock sympathy at the grey pallor of my face, delighted at the prospect that I would soon be larger than her.

Snatched phone calls, Snapchat messages, double-taps on Instagram and WhatsApp messages kept mine and Mike's relationship alive. I told myself that women survived their husband's absences in the army of up to a year and that Asian couples often found themselves thrown together in arranged marriages, with little in common other than their parents' business connections. Yet they still made it work! In comparison, Mike and I had the biggest connection anyone could ever have: a child. We had as good a chance as anyone …

Didn't we?

My twelve-week scan soon came however, and Mike was nowhere to be seen, for he had first year exams. Mum accompanied me instead and she cried as she regarded the blurry blob on screen. For a moment, I thought she was sad or ashamed, but moments later she was enveloping me in her bony embrace and telling me how proud she was of me. A little non-plussed by the sight of my baby on screen, hardly able to relate to the image, I accepted her words, sure the same sense of love and belonging my mother had for us would come to me later.

More time passed, and Mike became just a voice at the end of the phone, as my parents took it upon themselves to be there for me, instead. My usually small frame expanded rapidly. I was carrying the baby high and felt bent over backwards by the weight of the pregnancy. A twenty-week scan rolled around and it was confirmed I was carrying a boy. My Dad beamed from ear to ear, telling everyone he'd known all along the first Carmichael boy was on his way. My sisters cooed over the scan pictures and Hannah even tried crocheting a blue cardigan for the baby, though all she managed in the end was a wonky over-sized square, which she wrapped up for me anyway. I watched them all get excited and wondered when I would. All I felt was despair, clutching at my insides as I contemplated the future. What would become of me and Mike? What would become of this child?

What would become of me?

Thirteen

Mike arrived for an extended visit over the Easter Holidays. Mum insisted Amanda move in with the twins in their bedroom for the duration, much to my sisters' disgust. The baby's birth was imminent and I felt like I was the size of a house. This did not seem to stop Mike, who could not seem to keep his hands off me. It was like he was trying to get me all back for himself, having lost put to my family for so many months. Even though sex was the last thing on my mind, I felt grateful Mike did not find me disgustingly unattractive, nor see the 'whale' Sal did, which she would mutter under her breath whenever Mum was out of earshot.

But Mike's desire to control everything did not stop there. He began to badger me about the child's name. We were out on the patio and it was a pleasant and unusually warm April evening. Mum had told my sisters to give us some space and had warned them to stay off the patio on pain of death. Even so, Hannah could be seen watching us from her upstairs bedroom window, her face pressed against the glass in what she thought was a comical pose.

'I think… Dylan.' He said.

Irritation flooded through me: yet again, someone was deciding things for me!

'I don't like it.' I said out of sheer badness, even though I knew full well I had circled that particular name in the book Mum had given me.

'Okay,' Mike said, his tone measured, 'What about Jonathan?'

'Boring.' I declared and meant it, this time.

'You're choosing his name, then.' He said, deadpan. It was not a question.

'I'm carrying him. I have to give birth.' I said, my tone a little testy. 'Think of it like my reward. It's only fair.'

A shadow passed between us at that moment and the balance of power shifted to Mike as he regarded me, grinding his teeth together.

'The baby should have my surname, then.' He said.

I had never considered the idea before that moment. As far as I was concerned, the child would be a Carmichael. Same as me, same as my sisters. Mike had not even revealed whether he would ever support me and the baby financially, never mind commit to us or live with us.

'We'll see.'

'It's only fair.' Mike echoed.

'We're not married, though.' I said, bewildered.

'So?' Mike said, infuriatingly. How many times had I listened to him give that ridiculously childish retort to his own father? That decided it.

'The baby's having my surname.' I asserted.

The shadow that had passed between us the previous moment now seemed to leap out of Mike, across the patio. A bitter argument ensued and Mike kicked one of the patio chairs over. It fell onto the concrete with a metallic clatter that brought my mother running. Not seeing her in the kitchen doorway, Mike grabbed my arm and pulled me towards him, his thumb and forefinger dug in my flesh, painful as I tried to struggle out of his grasp as he repeated his demand: *the baby would have his surname.*

'What do you think you're doing?' My mother's voice was low – and dangerous.

But Mike did not know my mother and let go of my arm.

'Just a minor disagreement.'

My mother smiled, but I knew what was coming next. I had seen that smile dozens of times before, it had no humour attached to it whatsoever. If sharks were able to smile, they would look just like her.

'You're a bully, Michael.' My mother declared.

The colour drained from Mike's face as I felt mine flush read. I was handling this! She couldn't interfere, not again. But though I opened my mouth to speak, no sound came out. Mike just stood there, awkward, his face puzzled: he literally had no idea what my mother was talking about.

'Look, I don't know what you thought you saw…' Mike said.

'Silly boy,' My mother interrupted. 'I had your number the first time I met you. You're worse than a spoilt four-year-old.'

'Mum…!' I began. But a look from her silenced me and rage burned inside me. Mike was my boyfriend. I didn't need her protection. *I'm a big girl now!*

My father appeared from the kitchen, oblivious to the atmosphere. My mother turned to him, whilst keeping her iron gaze on Mike.

'Dan, do us a favour and take Michael home to his father's, will you? Keys are on the hook.'

'I thought Mike was staying until…' Dad started, then stopped. He caught up. '… Of course.'

I watched Mike slam his stuff into his bag, not saying a word, despite my garbled protestations that we should go downstairs and try and talk it through with my parents. I felt a kind of guilt but wasn't sure why. Mike had manhandled me, I hadn't asked for it. But I hadn't asked for Mum to step in either! I was pulled both ways: on one side, a mother too sure of herself to ever ask what I wanted or needed. On the other, an immature teenage boy who believed a test of love was whether I defied that mother for him. Yet this didn't have to be about sides.

Why couldn't everyone just meet me in the middle?

Mike stalked off with my father to the car, my mother insisting I stay back with her.

'I know you don't understand now,' she said, 'But I would be a bad mother if I let him do that.'

'You thought I would just let him?' I wanted to say, though my voice betrayed me once again, drying up in my mouth.

What would I have said or done, had my mother not put her foot down? I knew what Mike had done was wrong. I wasn't a child who needed to be told how men should treat women. He'd hurt me for daring to oppose him! But instead of trusting me to make that call, my mother had rushed in to save me, just like she always did. She had taken my power away from me when I needed to make a stand. Perhaps I would even have sent Mike back to his father's myself? Now we would never know.

The car door slammed shut and Dad drove Mike away.

Fourteen

A couple more weeks passed. Mike's texts and phone calls dwindled away to nothing under the weight of my mother's disapproval. She told my sisters what had happened and everyone assumed I would never see Mike again. Great! What about what I thought? It didn't seem to matter. Sal and Amanda told me I was weak and pathetic if I so much as heard out his apology. What did they know about relationships? Sal had never been kissed and the sum total of Amanda's experience involved a few drunken bunk-ups behind the youth centre in town with Billy Thompson, an apprentice car mechanic from my year at college.

I wondered how much my baby's future was being shaped against my will. I deserved to be able to make my own decisions for my own kid, without the pressure of my family, however well-meaning. But it was like I was trapped behind glass. No matter how much I banged and hollered, no one heard me.

My due date came and went. I was frustrated as hell, hot and uncomfortable. It was like waiting for the worst appointment in history: every dental appointment and exam, rolled into one. I dreaded it and wanted it over with.

Finally, about six days after the due date, I woke in the middle of the night to red hot pain and a large damp patch on the sheets. It lasted just a few moments but took my breath away. I couldn't even cry out. *Here we go*. I knew immediately it was labour. There was no turning back now. I had to go through this. *Oh, God!* Despite my fear, a part of me felt excitement. I would meet my baby at last. Then I realised: he still didn't have a name! What was I going to call him???

Amanda woke groggily to find me repacking my case for the hospital, checking and re-checking the babygros, nappies and other equipment in there.

She sat up, as if on a spring: 'Are you in labour?'

I nodded. Amanda ran out of the bedroom, yelling. Seconds later, my sisters were all crowded around me, my sleepy-eyed mother pulling clothes on over the top of her pyjamas. My Dad had been staying for the last few days 'just in case'. I was grateful for it now: Hannah and the twins looked more scared than me, their eyes wide. Even Sal and Amanda seemed sympathetic. I sensed there was something momentous at work here: I was about to become a mother. A new life was on the way. Whilst I had obviously known this all along, I had not felt it before.

Contractions started to come in earnest in the car. I discovered there was nothing more painful in the world than going round a roundabout when in labour. Mum kept glancing over from the front seat behind the wheel and saying stupid things like 'Breathe through it!' What the hell did that mean?? I shouted a few swear words at her I could never have got away with at any other time.

Mum was convinced I'd have the baby in the car, but once we got to the hospital a midwife confirmed it would be hours yet. I felt crushed by the lack of progress. I'd been sure being so young would mean I'd have the baby quickly. About ten hours in, I was asking for all the drugs available, despite having written in my birth plan I'd wanted only gas and air.

'You're doing really well,' Mum said.

Again, I was struck by the fact it was a ridiculous thing

to say. I was only doing what I had to! It wasn't like I could cancel the birth and do something else. But the sheer effort stopped me from yelling at her this time. I could only concentrate on delivering the baby.

Finally, over twenty hours after my waters first broke, a healthy baby boy arrived. He was smaller than I expected, even though the midwife said he was a good size, 'A little bruiser' she said, with a strong Scottish accent. The baby had huge eyes and even the same mole on his chin as Mike. I couldn't stop crying and Mum burst into tears as well.

The midwife took a picture on Mum's phone. 'What's his name?'

I'd expected to say 'I don't know' or 'I'll think of a name later'. Yet staring at my new son in my arms, a name came to me from thin air: 'Alex.'

Mum beamed. 'Good choice.'

I didn't want to stay in the hospital. Mum argued my case with the midwives: I was low risk; I had a big support network at home; I wanted to go home as soon as possible. But the midwives just smiled patronisingly. They advised us both we could go 'as soon as the doctor did her rounds'.

So, we ended up sitting around. I listened to the cries of new babies and the exhausted sighs of new mothers; I felt the frustration and envy of pregnant women still waiting for labour. Ambling up and down the corridor, bored, I was reminded of the sheep in the farms near our cottage, during lambing season. The ewes would stamp at us kids, warning us whenever we tramped through the fields. The women on the ward were just the same: *stay away from our babies.*

About three hours into our vigil, Mike turned up. The first I became aware of him was raised voices at the nurses' station. My mother had gone out to ask after the doctor again and run into him. He'd been ambling along the corridor, looking for me and the baby.

'She doesn't want to see you!'

I hobbled to the ward doorway, the baby in my arms. I would not go so far as ten steps away from the crib without him. I was surprised at how much I still hurt and how difficult walking was. In my naïve mind, I suppose I had thought that like the mothers I'd seen on television, I would deliver the baby and go bounding on my way.

'Mum.' I said, my tone delivering my message at last, several weeks too late: *I will handle this.*

Mike was standing his ground, a bunch of sorry-looking carnations in one hand, a teddy bear with a blue jumper on in the other. Mum regarded me with undisguised irritation.

'I'm going for a coffee.' She said to me, then looked at Mike, venom in her eyes. 'I'll be just down this corridor.'

Mike presented the flowers and teddy, awkward as ever. He fell back on platitudes like, 'well done' and 'he's gorgeous'. The words sounded wooden, automatic. I wanted to say something about what had happened on the patio, but didn't feel able to. On the most important day of our lives so far, we talked about nothing.

About twenty minutes later, Mike gave me a kiss on the cheek and was gone again. Mum stalked back in, eyeballing him on the way out. She started her demands straight away: *what was happening? Were we still together? What about access? Was he prepared to pay maintenance?*

'I don't know.' I replied, truthfully.

The double doors swung shut, as if Mike had never been there.

Fifteen

The first few weeks following Alex's birth passed in a blur. There were numerous visitors to the house. Shona was first, home from university for the weekend. She carried no present for the baby, just a giant litre bottle of vodka for me:

'You're gonna need this!'

Typical Shona.

A couple of old friends from college arrived with baby clothes and yet more teddies dressed in blue. I had lost touch with most of our old squad as they discovered their exciting new worlds, away from home for the first time. Most of the visitors were my Mum and Dad's friends, eager to see the first ever Carmichael boy. Lots of gifts arrived from people I didn't even know, along with a shower of congratulations. It was weird: would they have been so interested had the child been another girl? But I shoved these mean thoughts to the back of my mind. I smiled, sitting next to my mother as she showed off her first grandchild to anyone who spared five minutes, including the postman and even two tourists who had got lost.

Yet life moves on and what was new always becomes old, or at least normal. Even the twins lost their starry looks when regarding the baby, complaining instead he cried too much in the night. Alex was a colicky baby and slept only fitfully for an hour, here or there. I felt like a zombie, drifting through my life like I was watching myself from above. A few weeks into all this, Amanda announced she was moving out of our room and in with Sal and Hannah, permanently. An almighty argument ensued when Hannah was discovered raiding Amanda's beauty course stuff, which somehow became my fault as well. Breastfeeding proved more difficult than I hoped when Alex was so prone to colic, so despite my mother's and Sal's obvious disapproval, I put him on a bottle.

'He won't be as intelligent.' Sal declared one morning, as if infant nutrition was her speciality.

'Well how can he be intelligent anyway, if he's my kid?' I retorted, tired out from yet another night pacing up and down the bedroom floor with Alex. Sal rolled her eyes at me as usual and went back to her school books.

Motherhood wasn't quite as fulfilling as I hoped, either. I was bored. I suppose I'd thought I'd magically grow up, or at least know more, the moment I had Alex. Yet I felt the same as I always had, just more pressurised now. So much of motherhood was drudgery. Nappies. Feeding. Bathing. Cleaning. Washing. A never-ending cycle, going round and round. The fact I saw no one and knew no one going through parenting for the first time made me feel more isolated than ever. I cyber-stalked my old friends' pages and profiles, taking note of new names and faces. I was filled with jealousy over their exciting lives and photos. When my sisters came crashing through the doors of the house complaining about school or college and what had happened that day, I was envious.

I loved Alex … Of course I did. I would have done it all the same again, too. I didn't get it when I heard parents say anything different. How could they wish their kids had not been born? Even so, I just wanted to run away from it all, too. Life really seemed to be as much of a paradox as Shona had said, back when she was just eleven.

I had no clue what to do about it.

What felt like a million years and five minutes passed. Alex was sitting up; then on solids; then crawling and then walking. He took his first steps on his first birthday. He said his first word: 'Mama' (annoyingly, this was followed by 'Sal'). Each milestone was reached and noted as if it were completely natural: why shouldn't he? But still I worried about our future, what would come next for us. Would we be okay? Maybe all mothers felt this way. I wouldn't know. I hadn't done this before.

Alex was a mini human hurricane, able to get away with almost anything. My sisters and parents forgave him for spilling poster paint on the twins' beds; drawing on the walls; even cutting the hair off the tail of my mother's favourite cat, Monty. When he wasn't being naughty, Alex didn't appear to worry about missing out on his father's influence. Since the birth, Mike had seen him only a handful of times. We'd always met up in a backstreet café somewhere, since Mum had made it clear Mike was not welcome in her house. Alex never wanted to go to Mike, hiding behind me. I felt sorry for both of them, especially my Ex. He didn't know what to do, or what he was supposed to do. I could relate; I felt exactly the same.

Then the world as I knew it came crashing down.

Sixteen

It's hard to remember exactly where it started. Sal had been baiting me for weeks over Alex. Sal had discovered calling his development into question, cunningly disguised as 'concerns', were enough to rile me. She dug deep, finding as many as she could. Alex was apparently walking with his toes turned inward; he had a lisp; he had a below average vocabulary; I had apparently given him food too early, so now he was 'destined' for digestive problems and some cancers as an adult.

Even though I knew I had to rise above it, she never let up on the psychological warfare. When she suggested - for the millionth time! - that Alex's intelligence had been affected by me putting him on the bottle, there was an argument. I grabbed her by the collar, pleased momentarily by the fear in my sister's eyes. Shame followed, but I pushed the flat of both hands against her shoulders. Seated on a stool, she wind-milled both arms, but was unable to grab anything that would stop her fall. She sprawled on the kitchen tiles, hitting her lip against the side of the table as she went down. Sal, shocked by my actions - I don't think I had actually hit her before – touched her fingers to her lip. At the sight of the blood, she started crying.

'What have you done?'

Mum materialised in the kitchen, only after the event.

Rage coursed through me at my mother's words. Not,

'What's happened?' to both of us. Instead, *what had I done?* As usual, I was cast as the outsider, the potential trouble-maker, the cuckoo in the nest. And I was sick of it. I had been the one who'd had my life turned upside down; I was the one who had never been asked how I'd felt; I was the one expected to follow my mother's wishes and to some-how ignore even the most strategic and cruel sibling rivalry.

Enough was enough!

I threw Alex's belongings in a variety of black plastic bags. Mum first shouted and screamed. Then she pleaded with me, unable to understand why I'd suddenly flipped. The twins watched wide-eyed and Alex wailed at the atmos-phere, clinging to my leg and torn between us all. Unable to get through to me, Mum called Dad. He rushed over, trying to make me see sense. It didn't work.

Another phone call. Shona's dad was dispatched to pick me and Alex up (luckily Shona was at home from university for a so-called 'reading week'. This really meant she was at The Moon every night, getting hammered). The initial drama over, there was a half hour wait where I sat in the front room and listened to my Mother sobbing at the kitch-en table. Dad tried one last time with me, confused as ever. He reminded me of Mike, which made me want to go even more.

Finally, a car horn sounded outside: Shona's dad was here. I gathered my stuff together – just four paltry plastic bags of it – and loaded Alex into the pushchair. Mum and Dad came to the living room door. They made no effort to lift a finger and help. I knew they wouldn't. Despite my an-ger, I supposed I would have done the same if it was Alex. Yet I still felt unable to let go of the anger and resentment that had built up in me for so long. That paradox again.

'Bye.' My eyes were steely and cold.

'Where are you going?' Mum's voice was quieter than I had ever heard.

'Shona's.' I knew I should reassure her, but I felt powerful for the first time in years. How sad and mean was I?

'… And then?' Dad demanded.

I shrugged. I didn't have to do this, I knew that. I could come back in a few days and a line would be drawn under it. All I would have to do is admit I was wrong. All would be forgotten and life could trudge on as it was.

But there was another part of me that demanded my voice was heard. I couldn't live like this any longer. I was no longer just their eldest daughter. I was a mother myself now, I had to go out into the world and *be* that role. I could live life in limbo anymore; I had to go out and grab life by the balls at last. I had to make my own mistakes and they had to let me.

I struggled out to the car. Shona's dad helped me load the bags and the pushchair into the back. He took forever testing Alex's car seat. As I waited, Sal plucked up her nerve and ran out the front of the house.

'Don't go.' She said breathlessly.

'I have to.' I willed her to apologise, to admit she was in the wrong too.

Sal's face twisted. I thought she was about to cry. I wanted to throw my arms around her, despite how she'd treated me over the years. But the moment was over in a micro-second.

'This is typical of you!' Confrontational Sal was back, her lip curled in that sneer of hers.

I smiled. 'No, that's the point… It isn't.'

Without another word, I got in the back of the car, next to Alex. As Shona's dad turned the key in the ignition, the sound brought Mum and the rest of the family to the porch. They all looked so miserable and a part of me ached to be with them. But I knew I couldn't go back. Not now. I waved. Like sad reflections of myself, they copied, unable to understand what had really happened or why I was leaving.

I had to do this.

Shona's dad's expensive car bombed down the country lanes too fast. For the first time in ages I felt as if I could breathe properly. I still didn't know what would come next, but now I felt excited, as well as worried. I would need to find somewhere to live and make some decisions – especially about jobs and education - but I was no longer in limbo.

My destiny was my own at last.

In my pocket, the tell-tale vibration of an incoming call roused me from my thoughts. In the car seat next to me, Alex was already asleep, thumb in mouth. I hesitated before answering, feeling sure it would be Mum. The call died but began ringing again immediately. I sighed, taking the phone from my pocket. My eyes bugged out in surprise. It was not Mum.

On the screen flashed the name: MIKE ...

Mike

'The guys who fear becoming fathers don't understand that
fathering is not something perfect men do,
but something that perfects the man. The end product of
child-raising is not the child, but the parent.'
Frank Pittman

Seventeen

The world shifted again. Sound went first, like drop-out on a bad phone signal. Then there was a weird interruption like white noise, shocking in its suddenness. Imagery flashed past my eyes, quick as a city landscape through a train window. As the images reeled past, I could see everyone there was someone I knew. They moved their arms in jerky circles, backwards and forwards and nonsensical, like nightclub dancers under strobe lighting.

Next: nothing.

'… Lizzie, you there?'

Mike's voice cut through the darkness, clear and obvious.

My hand appeared in front of me, disembodied, that positive pregnancy tester gripped in my fingers. The rest of me appeared, blinking back to existence as if I had never been away. The phone was to my ear; I stood in front of the aluminium mirror, shell-shocked. I took a deep breath like a swimmer breaking the surface of dark water after a dive into the murky depths.

'Yes.' My voice hoarse; it rasped in my throat.

I looked around those toilets again, wondering what had prompted such a strong reaction in me. It couldn't just have been the positive pregnancy test… Could it? I recalled one of my mother's magazines: there had been a story about a woman whose health had been badly affected by pregnancy and she'd had a brain haemorrhage. But the woman had been both middle-aged and hugely pregnant, her blood pressure had sky-rocketed. It couldn't be that for me; I had been pregnant only a matter of days. Besides, I was only young.

'… I said we'd meet them at seven.' Mike said.

I realised I had heard nothing prior to that moment. He seemed pretty chilled. That meant only one thing: Mike was planning a night out. It was the only time he was ever happy: if he could get drunk or stoned and play pool, life made sense to him. Despair flooded through me: *Mike was my Dad!* How could I have not recognised that until this moment?

'I can't,' I spluttered.

The toilets seemed so small, the dirty walls and their juvenile graffiti felt far too close. Heat worked its way up my neck and down my back. Breath felt like it was catching in my chest: I couldn't gather enough air.

'You alright?'

'I'm fine.'

I grabbed my bag and stumbled towards the doors of the toilets, pushing it open with my shoulder, phone still to my ear. Fresh air rushed in, almost shocking me back to life, rejuvenating me in an instant. I could breathe again. I could think straight!

… I stopped.

Beyond the toilets, the marketplace was deserted. I gazed around the big, open car park in surprise. There were no stalls, no crowds. Just rows and rows of cars: battered old bangers mostly, broken up by sparkling Landrovers and Jeeps with bull bars, the Yummy Mummies from on the big estates at the back of town drove. Yet it was Wednesday, market day. Where had everyone gone?

'Where are you?' Mike said, as if he could read my mind.

'I'm in town.'

I was keen to get off the line. I could feel my confession rising in my mouth now like bile. I was sure I'd spill my guts over the phone. Mike's dad's house was just two or three streets from where I was standing, but I couldn't face making the five-minute walk to Francis' to tell Mike there. I could just see the old man's face, always impassive, yet somehow able to transmit his disapproval. He'd never liked me. The girl with the rag-tag family, I was not good enough for his boy. But Francis was not good enough for Mike, either. We'd all been mismatched.

'Come over.' Mike said.

I knew immediately what he had on his mind.

'No. We need to talk.'

We need to talk. What a clichéd phrase. It was up there with, 'I will never leave you'. Everyone left. Mike's mother. My father. My mother was so used to it now, she had stopped depending on Dad altogether. She took in ironing and did cleaning jobs like at the holiday chalets; the twins would trail after her and squirt air freshener in their wake. In the summer months we were usually okay, money-wise. But the winter months were harsh. The holiday chalets would close up and Dad was usually let go from whatever hotel he had taken up residence in that year. Sometimes Mum would take pity on him and let him sleep on the sofa in the run up to Christmas, making him pull his weight as Daddy Daycare whilst she looked for work. Unlike him, Mum had a few qualifications and occasionally she'd find temping work in offices. It was always strange to see my mother in a shirt and skirt, her frizzy hair tied up in a bun.

Shona's dad spent all his time working, away from the family and away from his marriage, too. He preferred the company of women whose services he paid for. Shona's mum pretended she didn't know when she reviewed the monthly credit card bill. Shona had seen the bill on the counter once and Googled the names of the companies listed. As well as being majorly grossed-out, Shona had ago-nised for hours with me: she wondered if she should tell her mother? I wasn't sure.

But then Shona had caught her mother Googling the names of the companies just as she had done, then log off. Shona had waited on tenterhooks all week for her father's return, sure there would be a major row when he did. In-stead, Shona's mother had merely welcomed Philip back. They had all sat the table together and eaten, just as they always did.

Shona told me she thought she would explode at first. But as her food went cold on her plate in front of her, Shona noted the distance between her parents: in the same room, yet so many miles apart. Shona excused herself and went to her room for the rest of the night, YouTube on full blast to hide her crying.

Then there was Nora, my mother's teacher friend. She'd had a husband who'd waltzed her down the aisle after a whirlwind romance of moonlight and roses. Hannah and the twins had even been bridesmaids. Yet just six months later he was gone, leaving Nora for another woman at the school. Feeling shamed and humiliated just for taking a chance, Nora had applied for every job she could at other schools but got none of them. She'd been forced to watch the pair of them getting lovey-dovey over the stale biscuits in the staffroom. *Ugh.*

I must admit, I didn't get it. Nora was cute, good-look-ing; the second wife was plump and plain. I heard Nora tell Mum she'd felt sure that once that honeymoon period of six months was up, her Ex would realise his mistake and at least move on, leaving the husband-stealer in the lurch, as she deserved. But even worse, the second wife lasted the distance, leaving Nora with never-ending questions: *what had she done – or not done? What was it about Nora, which had meant the Ex had felt he could just throw her away like that?*

Then there had been the Hutchinsons. They'd occupied the biggest, most splendid house, 'Hollyhocks', which had been up on the hill, above the village. It was a huge manor, with eight bedrooms, a paddock, two horses and a well-stocked garden, with its own gardener. The Hutchinsons were the couple who had everything. So it was all the more shocking, when the villagers woke up to the news that Mr. Hutchinson had put a shotgun in his mouth and pulled the trigger. It turned out that Mr. Hutchinson's fortune had been wiped out overnight by the stock exchange (though none of us kids had a clue what that meant). Feeling unable to tell his young wife, Mr. Hutchinson had decided suicide was his only option, forgetting the act left his large life insurance policy invalid. Mrs. Hutchinson was left with nothing. Hollyhocks had since been bought by a developer and turned into the holiday chalets my mother cleaned. Mum always complained of a chill to chalet number twenty-six, which was on the very spot the stable blocks had been, where Mr. Hutchinson had blown his brains out.

Then there was Mrs. Darby. She would always go on about 'family' and 'community', but Mrs Darby was all alone. There was no Mr. Darby and hadn't been for over thirty years. When they'd found out Mrs. Darby couldn't have kids, Mr. Darby just upped and left... According to Phyllis at the post office, anyway. Something inside me then felt sorry for Mrs. Darby then, even if she was an interfering old bag.

But Phyllis had had no luck either: she'd met her husband when she was just fourteen, younger than I was now. They'd enjoyed fifty wonderful years together and raised two children. Then, on the brink of retirement and a promised round the world trip together, Phyllis' husband had died of a heart attack. There had been no warning signs. He had been a healthy man of normal weight, even running the London Marathon twice for charity. Now, like the others, Phyllis was all alone in the world. Her two grown up children had families of their own, plus they had long since moved away in search of work. Now there was little room for Phyllis in their busy lives. Phyllis was lucky if she saw her grandchildren once or twice a year.

So, if 'I will never leave you' was untrue (I totally believed it was), then 'we need to talk' really meant, 'I have something to tell you and you're not going to like it'. So did Mike. I could feel the change in his demeanour, even down the phone: sudden guardedness with an air of panic:

'You breaking up with me?'

'No.' I said hastily, 'Nothing like that. I just... I just really need to see you.'

'Then come over.'

I knew I couldn't. If I went in Francis' house, my voice would fail me. At Mike's, in his attic bedroom with the tiny window and posters of Star Wars and Bruce Lee, I could pretend I was lovable, that Mike and I were meant to be together and life could be normal.

But I couldn't pretend today. Not about this.

'Meet me at Teddy's.' I said.

Eighteen

The Teddy Bear's Picnic was a twee little tourist trap in town, with gingham tablecloths and toadstool salt and pepper pots. At the back, there was a giant, colourful mural of toys all enjoying themselves. It was hardly the place someone like Mike would want to be seen. But The Moon would not be open yet and even if it were, his friends might be there playing pool. I needed to be able to talk to Mike alone, with no potential interruptions.

A car horn blasted at me. I realised I was still standing in the middle of the market car park, in one of the remaining spaces next to the clock tower. A huge beast of a car with a heavily-coiffured and impatient lady behind the wheel. There was a pink car seat in the back, a PRINCESS ON BOARD sign in the rear window. I wondered if the sign related to the driver or the little girl in the car seat.

'Okay, okay!'

Normally I would have skulked out the way, my cheeks red with shame, but I was beyond caring. I moved on, but not before I gave the driver The Finger, delighting for a moment in the perfect 'o' of her surprised, over-lip-glossed, fuchsia pink lips.

Walking through town, I saw why the market place had been empty: there was a demonstration on. Led by market people and marketgoers, banners carried slogans against a supermarket chain. I dodged demonstrators and their whistles and drums. There was a seemingly endless throng of people with signs, plus men and women with toddlers in pushchairs and on their shoulders.

It was peaceful, but noisy as hell. A tall woman with a megaphone kept yelling, over and over again the same slogan: 'No ifs! No buts! We will not let our market shut!' Policemen and women in neon yellow jackets watched over the demonstration, filtering people through the agreed routes and directing those who were lost or had been separated from friends and colleagues. A local news crew had set up their cameras and was filming, the cameraman slack-jawed and bored, chewing gum as he waited for the crowd to pass. I wondered where they had all come from.

Then I was out the other side of the crowd, into the dark side street where Teddy's was. The place was dead: a girl about my age in a black and dark red uniform lolled behind the counter, scrolling through her phone. She barely looked up as I entered. I sat down on a table near the back and stared at the famous mural. I noticed for the first time how faded it was. Over the years, chairs had hit the wall as they'd been scraped back, again and again. A ragdoll on the left was missing half her face.

'Yes, what can I get you?' The girl appeared by my table as if by magic, her expression bored and disinterested.

I looked at the coffee and tea menu on a chalkboard. It was hung at an angle above the counter. My stomach roiled at the thought of either. Perhaps the pregnancy was affecting me already. *Who knew? Not me.*

'Just a water.'

'Water.' The girl said, unimpressed. 'Fizzy or still?'

'Whatever, I don't care.' I snapped.

The girl rolled her eyes and retreated back behind the counter, slamming a glass and a sealed bottle of water next to me seconds later. At least I knew she hadn't spat in it.

I figured Mike would keep me waiting for making him

get out of bed. I wasn't wrong. About twenty-five minutes after I'd got to the tearooms, he shuffled across the threshold and fell into a chair opposite me.

'Let's have it, then.' He eyeballed me, as if daring me to speak.

I wondered how to break it to him. Was it best to just come out with it, or to try and couch it as gently as possible?

'Do you want a coffee?' I enquired.

'No. I do not want a coffee.' Mike replied, his fury bubbling under. 'I want to know what this is all about?'

I noticed he was wearing his best shirt, the one with the dragon on the righthand pocket. Even more curious for Mike, the shirt was ironed. His hair was still wet and brushed, for once. There was even the tell-tale whiff of aftershave wafting its way across the table at me. I smiled. He must have figured if he was going to get dumped, he might as well do it in style. I felt sorry for him in that moment and yet touched. Had the situation been reversed, I would have done exactly the same. What an odd moment to discover something in common between us both at last.

'I'm pregnant.'

Mike's eyes grew wide and his nostrils flared in alarm, rather like a spooked horse. I expected him to rise up angrily like one too, so steeled myself against the onslaught I felt sure was coming my way: *how could this have happened? Are you trying to trap me? Why didn't you take the morning after pill?*

Though the retorts to the first two questions were obvious, I did not have all the answers. Why *hadn't* I taken the morning after pill? I didn't have anything against it. Yet I had not got one, the night after we had not used contraception. But then, Mike helped me find or buy one, either. The morning after, he had not mentioned anything, but simply complained of a hangover. I could not face going to the doctor's and figured they'd only keep me waiting. It was impossible to get an appointment in this town and by the time I was seen, the seventy-two-hour deadline for the pill's effectiveness would probably have passed, anyway.

I supposed it had boiled down to one thing: money, or rather, lack of it. Though it might be available over the counter at pharmacies – about twenty pounds – I didn't have twenty pounds. I figured the odds were on my side. Female fertility in a twenty-eight-day cycle was just a two to three-day window per month, according to the internet. I surely was in one of those other twenty-five days, anyway? And even if I wasn't, that didn't mean I'd automatically get pregnant. So, I'd figured: *it had only been the once.* The chances were good (excellent, even!) that we would be lucky. We could just forget about that one, tiny drunken mistake.

Yet here we were.

'Say something, then.' I said at last.

'What do you want me to say?'

Fury coursed in my veins. I could not believe it. This was happening to *me*, yet he couldn't even ask how I felt? Even the anger I'd expected would have been better. Mike just sat there. He stared to the side of my head, not making eye contact, as if mesmerised by a dirty scuff mark on the wall. Behind the counter, the girl wiped the sideboards in lazy circles, pretending not to watch us.

I swallowed down my own fury. 'So, what do we do?'

Another blank expression from Mike. For one terrible moment, I thought he was going to say, 'No, you mean what do *you* do?' and then leave. But he sat before me, motionless. He wasn't going to bolt for the door, but that made the weird non-reaction all the stranger: how was I supposed to take it? I tried to rearrange the question, to gain a response.

'What do you want to do?'

Mike's tone was flat. 'Whatever you want to do.'

Despair turned to joy turned to confusion inside me in an instant. Was Mike saying he would stand by me regardless of my decision? I couldn't be sure. Were there conditions attached? Mike was so changeable. I didn't know whether I could rely on him. Did I want this baby? Even I wasn't sure.

Resentment bloomed again in my chest: he was putting everything on me! It wasn't fair. This was huge: the biggest thing either of us had ever had to face. I'd fulfilled my part of the deal; I had told him right away. But now he wouldn't tell me what he thought about it. How could I know what was the 'right' answer, if he would not tell me his own feelings on the matter?

'I don't know what I want to do.' I said, hoping this would prompt him into saying what he actually wanted.

Mike caught the eye of the girl behind the counter and said, 'Cappuccino, please. And…?' He looked to me, expecting me to order. When I didn't, he shot me one of his derisive looks and then smiled to the girl, just as quick. 'That's it. Cheers.'

The high-pitched whizz of the cappuccino frother filled the silence between us. Then Mike's order was placed in front of him with as much care as my water. Froth went over the side, onto the table. Mike was usually the type to complain or even demand another, but instead today he opened sugar packet after sugar packet, dumping the contents in his drink. Then he stirred it. Round and round and round, more froth spilling over the lip of the cup.

'Will you just stop?' I hissed.

Mike let the spoon fall abruptly from his hand, clanging the ceramic cup and saucer. 'What do you want from me?'

Seriously?? A bitter laugh caught in my throat. 'How about some emotional support?'

He shrugged. 'All a bit late now.'

'What is?' I said, my voice raising at last.

The girl behind the counter had stopped pretending she wasn't listening. She stared openly, like we were on one of those reality TV shows. I wanted to go over, slap her across the face. But I knew it was Mike I was mad with, really.

'I didn't do this by myself, you know. For God's sake Mike, I'm from a family of *six kids*. What did you expect?'

As soon as I uttered those words, I knew their truth. I was from a big family. Why hadn't it ever occurred to me, before? Sex had always been just a game between me and Mike. We had never thought it could have real consequences. There had even been times when we'd seen little kids in the park and exclaimed over how cute they were, how nice it would be to have our own. None of it had seemed real. We'd been play-acting, all along.

But Mike still sat in front of me, that blank expression etched into his features. He had no clue what to do, nor did he feel any need to come up with a plan. Faced with that, I did what I always did: I tried to fix the situation, even though it was going to pieces in front of my eyes.

'Okay… okay. Let's think about this logically.' I heard myself say, though my voice seemed to belong to someone else. 'If we had the baby, we could still go to university? I'll get my results, go through clearing, we can go to the same one instead. We can find a flat, live together… You, me and the baby. Maybe I can do my course part-time?'

I waited for Mike to agree or disagree. He shifted in his chair and pushed his sugar-laden cappuccino away, undrunk. 'I don't think we should make any hasty decisions.'

'Results come out in a few days!' I countered, 'If I'm to get into your uni, we need to sort this right away… We don't have any time to waste?'

But Mike still said nothing, his expression still blank. There was an awkward silence. A cheated smile played on my lips as realisation hit.

'You don't want to go to the same uni or live together, do you?'

Mike averted his gaze. 'I never said that.'

'No, you're not saying anything!' Cold anger replaced

my initial hot fury. 'You want me to have an abortion, is that it?'

He sighed. 'It's an option.'

For some reason, those words were like a dagger in my heart. Not because I was against abortion – I still wasn't sure whether I wanted the baby myself – but because Mike so obviously wasn't bothered in making any plans with me. I had believed we would be able to talk it over, if not as a couple, then at least as mates.

But it seemed like Mike had no such thought on his mind. He wanted the situation dealt with by whatever means, which I was to decide alone. All so he could continue in his life without interruption … And to Hell with me.

Well, to Hell with him.

Nineteen

I grabbed my bag and rose from my place. Without another word, I stalked out of Teddy's. Mike followed me, demanding to know what was wrong. Before we could turn the corner on to the high street, the girl from behind the counter had caught up with us. She badgered Mike for the money for the water and cappuccino, though I didn't stop. Mike threw change at her in irritation as I left them both behind.

I turned back on to the high street, finding myself back in the throng of the demonstration. Its din surrounded me, though it was dying off as it approached the town hall. Local council workers were waiting on the steps in readiness for the petition that would be presented to them by the tall woman with the megaphone. I wondered if the supermarket everyone was opposing was really such a bad thing. Wasn't there room for both the large store *and* the marketplace? The supermarket could also mean more work for the townspeople. When so many people had to leave Winby to search for work, it seemed odd for so many to actively go against work offered on their doorstep. They'd even cancelled trading to make that stand! I was reminded of Shona's talk of choices and paradoxes aged eleven and wondered, not for the first time, if we lived in the craziest place on Earth.

As I wandered back out of the crowd, I wasn't sure where I was going. All I knew was I couldn't go home. I was so wound up, I would immediately spill my guts to Mum. Then she would take over, just like she always did. I needed to make this decision myself.

Mike had made it clear he wasn't interested and wasn't going to help me. I felt a sick dread in the pit of my stomach. I wished I could somehow travel backwards in time and never even see Mike that night I got pregnant. But another part of me insisted I was strong; I could handle this, whatever I chose to do. And I did have a choice, didn't I? I didn't *have* to have this baby. But I didn't have to get rid of it, either. All I had to do was decide what it was I wanted and how I would handle it. Two different decisions… yet I could only choose one.

Both seemed so huge.

My phone rang in my pocket. I knew without even looking at the screen it would be Mike at the end of the line. Wanting to believe he might regret his behaviour at Teddy's, I put the phone to my ear and answered. He didn't say hello, so nor did I.

'Don't do this.' Mike said.

'Do what?'

'What you always do, Lizzie!' Mike sounded like a child whose toys had been taken away from him. 'Always, everything is my fault.'

'That's not true. All I wanted was some support.' I said, careful to keep my voice level. 'And what did I get? Nothing! As usual.'

'This has to be your decision.'

I caught sight of my cynical smile via my reflection in a shop window. 'Don't make out you're thinking of me. You wouldn't even say what you want!'

'You've never cared what I want before.' He spat.

I rolled my eyes. 'Quit feeling sorry for yourself. I literally asked you, you wouldn't answer. That's on you. You wouldn't even look me in the eye … And I've figured out why. You know what I'm like, you know I'll walk away.

Problem solved!'

'How can you say that?'

Mike sounded as if he were on the verge of tears. But those tears were not for me, or the pregnancy, or even the argument we were having. They were for himself. I could picture him: there was no traffic noise from his end of the line. I realised why: he would be back at home already. He'd retreated to his attic bedroom, Little Big Man hidden away from the scary world.

I decide to try one last time. 'So, what is it you want?'

More silence on the other end of the phone. I sighed.

'And there's my answer.'

I hung up, turning the phone on silent (for some reason I could never turn it off totally). I slipped the handset back in my coat pocket. I'd thought I wouldn't be able to rely on Mike, but it stung to have it confirmed. I just wished he'd have the guts to actually say it. But Mike couldn't help it. Francis could give nothing away, not even a hug. When Mike left their house, Francis would give his son a strange, cursory pat on the shoulder with those yellowed fingers of his; not even his whole palm, as if Mike were some kind of pet. Each time I had seen it happen, I had felt sorry for them both. Even Sal would hug me sometimes.

At the end of the high street, the road dipped steeply towards Roslin Road, the street down on the sea front which housed most of the town's small hotels and B&Bs. Orange shop fronts and old, tattered awnings gave them all a sad, ancient look more akin to old people's homes than luxurious places to stay. A forest of VACANCIES signs had popped up. It was high season, but it had it been a bad year.

I stopped outside one, The Belle View. I wandered up the steps and into reception without running into anyone: the small counter was deserted and beyond the internal window. I could see an old man, Pablo, asleep in his chair, his feet resting on a forest of paperwork. Pablo was from Barcelona and had travelled over to England in the seventies, a tale he'd tell anyone after a few whiskies. He hated Britain and its 'crazy people', but he hated Spain more (for reasons he would never disclose, no matter how drunk he got). The locals called Pablo 'Manuel' after the character in that old sitcom *Fawlty Towers* behind his back. Unlike Manuel, Pablo actually owned The Belle View and was razor sharp (when he wasn't asleep on the job).

A Polish cleaner eyed me suspiciously as I passed her vacuuming the deserted guest lounge. She didn't call me back as I made my way towards the steep stairs that led down to the kitchens. I didn't call ahead. I guess I wasn't sure if he'd even want to see me. I didn't have a plan, or even know what I was going to say.

I just wanted to see my Dad.

Twenty

I heard the crash of broken crockery, followed by an explosion of swearing as I approached the swing door: Dad was definitely on duty. Today it sounded as if he was on his own. I slipped inside the small kitchen. He had his back to me. He swept broken pieces of ceramic up, propelling them with the broom across the floor like hockey pucks into a cardboard box, congratulating himself every time he scored.

The kitchen was tiny: it was dominated by a massive, single hob with two ovens underneath. The Belle View did only bar snacks in the afternoon and at night, so it was for the morning breakfasts. Next to the ovens was a large sink, two large coffee and tea urns awkwardly jammed next to it on the other side. The rest of the kitchen was aluminium racks held plates and cups, piled in huge Tower-of-Pisa-style stacks, threatening to topple over if you walked too close.

The Belle View had been one of the few hotels that had re-employed my Dad after a single season, so I knew the hygiene there was poor: look underneath those racks and you'd find thick piles of dust hair and food, even the occasional mouse. Once I had witnessed a chef called Wes drop a rasher of bacon off the hob and chase it underneath one such rack. He then fished it out and rinsed it under the tap, slamming it back on the hob for a few moments before shoving it on an outgoing to plate to the dining room. Obviously, I had refused any offers of food out of that kitchen ever since. Dad still ate there most days though and had never even had so much as a stomach upset.

'Lizzie!' Dad turned and noticed me at last and abandoned the broom, letting it fall where he stood. He was all smiles. 'To what do I owe this pleasure?'

I'd just wanted to see a familiar, friendly face and avoid the interrogation I knew was waiting for me back home. I burst into tears. Dad nearly fell over the broom as he rushed over to hug me, cooing at me like I was four years old. This would have normally irritated the hell out of me, but I was glad to accept after Mike's non-reaction earlier. We stood there for a good while, saying nothing. I felt my tears sink into Dad's chef's jacket that smelled of rancid old bacon and that horrible aftershave he insisted on buying off the market.

'Going back to the flat.' Dad barked at Pablo on our way past reception.

Pablo was awake now, working his way through a trillion invoices, all stamped OVERDUE. 'Oh no you don't, mister!'

Pablo called everyone 'mister' or 'missus'; he didn't seem able to retain anyone's name or surname. This worked as a system until a friend of mine from college, Dusty, had started at the Belle View. Though male, with his long hair, pierced ears and impressive eye make-up, there were many who couldn't decide if Dusty was a girl or not. Including Pablo: Dusty got called both 'mister' and 'missus', dependant on the day.

'Family emergency.'

'Not off 'til six!' Pablo shrieked.

'Stick it up your arse.' Dad ushered me out.

Despite my despair at my situation, I could not help a tiny smile. I was used to Dad automatically folding whenever Mum went on the rampage. I hadn't seen this side of him before. Helpless, Pablo watched Dad leave.

The Belle View's staff accommodation was directly be-hind the hotel itself: once it had been a large garage but it was now divided into six flats on two levels. Pablo and his wife Marta occupied the plush one at the front on the ground floor, with Marta's daughter Flo in the second nic-est with her sons Harvey and Oliver. They shared the small patch of garden between the flats and the hotel. The remain-ing four were tiny little studio flats crammed next to one another on the second floor.

Being the kitchen porter and bottom of the pecking order (even after the chambermaid), Dad had the smallest. This didn't seem to bother him though. Inside, the studio flat was as small as it looked. There were no framed pictures on the walls, just a collection of pictures on a pin board over the futon: me, the others, my Mum, a dog my father had as a boy. There was no one else: no friends, no busty pin ups, not even my Dad's own long deceased parents. My Dad was every inch the only child, meandering through life more or less alone. He didn't see the need for anyone else, like he'd picked my mother up by accident along the way. Us kids had popped up, one by one, but Dad had continued ever for-wards … Yet paradoxically stayed in the same place. *How was that even possible?*

'Do you want a cup of tea?' Dad said and then in the same breath: 'Probably not. First thing your mother always went off, how I always knew.'

'Are you ashamed of me?' I said.

Dad's eyes grew as wide as Mike's for a moment and I was sure he was about to say 'yes'.

'No!' He insisted. 'Of course not. These things happen.'

He sat down in a bean bag chair, started rolling a mas-sive joint, then thought better of it and abandoned the pa-pers and baccy in the ashtray.

'I don't know what to do.' I collapsed onto another bean

bag.

My Dad smiled. 'You know, it wasn't that long ago I had this conversation with your mother. About you.'

'Do you regret it?' I winced, dreading the answer.

'No. How could I?' I could see in his eyes he was telling the truth. My Dad was many things –a bit of a waster being just one – but he was no liar. 'What does Mike say?'

'Nothing.' I said, unable to contain my bitterness.

Dad pursed his lips rather like Mum would. 'Little scrote. Never liked him.'

I looked at Dad in surprise. 'Why didn't you say so?'

Dad shrugged. 'What good would that have done? The more we'd have hated him, the more you would've liked him. I was a teen myself once, you know.'

I sighed. 'I haven't told Mum yet.'

'But you will.' Dad said, unconcerned. And I knew he was right. I couldn't allow a complicated decision like this to come around and not involve her.

'She'll want me to keep the baby.'

'She'll want you to do what's best for you.' Dad asserted.

'I wish…' I started.

But Dad shushed me. 'Don't wish your life away. Things happen. Sometimes good, sometimes bad, sometimes unexpected. We just have to do what we can and deal with them.'

I wondered where this philosophical side of my Dad had come from. For so many years, I had supposed he thought of so little but getting stoned, having a laugh and winding my Mum up by being so flaky.

Dad leaned forward, grabbed my hand. 'I know I've not been the best Dad, love. I've been crap, actually. But whatever you decide – and I mean *whatever* – I'm behind you one hundred per cent. You got that?'

Mute, I nodded. Dad grinned.

'That's my girl.' He said.

Twenty-one

Dad and I ordered a takeaway and ate it, streaming comedy box sets. Dad promised he'd go with me to tell Mum in the morning. After Mike, I felt relieved and not so alone. So, for a few hours, I relaxed and remembered what I loved about my Dad. I'd been so angry with him for so long, I'd forgotten. But he was funny and witty, able to quote movies he hadn't seen for years; plus, his ability to burp on demand was legendary. I was able to enjoy the moment for what it was, without dreading the following morning and Mum.

Watching TV with Dad, I felt an ache in my guts. I put it down to nerves, or maybe eating the greasy Chinese take-away on an empty stomach. But later that night, I woke on the futon with my knees up against my chest as pain erupted in my belly. It was so sharp, for a moment it took my breath away. Just as swiftly, that terrible, spiking pain disappeared and I was able to sit up. Black spots sprang up in my vision. Nausea hit me next, flooding my mouth and the back of my throat with sour saliva. *What was wrong with me?*

Dad was asleep in the beanbag chair, his head thrown back like a child, mouth open and catching flies. With difficulty, I got up. I lurched past him towards the tiny bathroom, locking the door behind me. I leant against the door, trying to breathe slowly and deeply, but taking in only the stale air from the windowless cubicle. Again, that awful pain gripped me but this time it was worse. It made me double over, preventing me from crying out; only an animalistic whimper made its way out of me. Those spots in my vision seemed to grow and I wondered for a nanosecond if I would black out. Then the pain rushed in again and this time I uttered a single, low guttural howl.

'Lizzie?' My dad was awake and pounding on the door. '... Lizzie!'

Woozy, I sat on the toilet. I didn't have enough wherewithal to answer. I knew instinctively what was happening. Moments later, I confirmed it as I peeled off the pyjama bottoms my dad had given me.

Blood.

Horror-struck, I made one single observation before Dad broke the door down. It was not like period blood, which was typically dark crimson in colour. This was bright red, like if you cut your own hand or arm with a knife. Life blood.

'Oh God, Lizzie. Lizzie!'

There was a crash as the door yielded. Dad was in the room. I was only peripherally aware of him and the fact I didn't even have anything on my bottom half. For some reason I didn't even care, normally I would be mortified. I had worse things to worry about: all I could concentrate on was the blackness that threatened to invade me, take me over. I knew I had to keep it away or I would be lost.

I tried to stand, but my knees buckled. Dad grabbed me and wrapped me in a towel, running out on to the flat balcony with me in his arms like a small child. He was shouting, pleading, but his voice seemed so far away.

There were more shouts and slammed doors. Flo's husband Jonno appeared on the balcony, yelling for Pablo. The small Spaniard came running in a dressing gown and slippers, holding keys to one of the hotel vans. Dad grabbed them and shoved me in the passenger's seat.

'You'll be okay, baby. You'll be okay.' Dad said, turning

the key in the ignition. And I wondered why he would say that because it was obvious I was losing the baby.

Until I realised he was talking to me.

Then I passed out.

Twenty-two

Ectopic pregnancy, doctors said: when a fertilised egg tries to develop outside the uterus, in the fallopian tube. They'd broken it to me they'd to take my tube as well. They told me later I'd been very lucky, but I didn't feel lucky. It was unusual in someone in my age, they said, but not unheard of. *Just my luck, typical me.*

In the hospital, I regarded the small, keyhole scar next to my bellybutton and was reminded of one of my mother's cats when she was spayed. She had had a similar scar, made obvious where they had shaved her fur away. No fur to grow back and hide mine, either. I wondered what it would do to my chances of having a baby when I wanted one, then caught myself. Twelve hours ago, I'd been pregnant, not sure if I even wanted to be. Now I was thinking about kids in the future. *Wow.*

I was only in hospital a short time, but there were visitors. All the family crowded around my bed. The devastated, put-a-brave-face-on-it smile of my mother; the wide eyes of my sisters and the sympathetic glances of my dad, the only one who really knew what had happened or my doubts about the pregnancy in the first place. There was a part of me that felt relief the situation had been taken out of my hands: I had felt too young to deal with such a huge decision, especially when Mike had basically told me he wanted nothing to do with it. But weirdly, at the same time,

I felt cheated. It had been my choice to make ... Yet before I could decide, it had been snatched from my hands. It wasn't fair!

Just before I was due to leave, Mike arrived at the hospital. My parents and sisters made themselves scarce, so we could talk. Mike brought a large bouquet with him, probably bigger than he could afford, when he didn't have a Saturday job. I wondered if he had taken Francis' credit card again but accepted the blooms with a murmured 'thank you.' Mike was awkward and embarrassed, making veiled enquiries about how I was. I wondered if he would talk about what we'd said in Teddy's, but ten minutes into the clumsy exchange it was clear he was not going to. Just like at the café, I realised he was going to skirt around the subject, sweep it aside and hope for the best.

'I could have died, you know.'

'I know.' Mike averted his gaze from mine, as if he couldn't handle what I was saying. But what was new? He stared at the floor, tapping it with his foot like a child caught out.

'I don't think you do.' I said coldly. 'I don't think you care.'

'How can you say that?' He wailed for the second time in just a few days.

'I bet your first thought was, 'thank God for that'?'

'No... no.' His reply was unconvincing. 'I was worried about you!'

'I wish I could believe that.' I said.

'We can still go to the same university.' He pleaded, 'We can live together, if you like?'

I couldn't believe it. Was he for real? It had not occurred to me Mike would think we could find our way back from his non-reaction in the café. I'd asked for his help and he'd basically slammed a metaphorical door in my face. Yet days later here he was, saying everything could go back to normal, as long as I made the decision again! But I knew I would never feel the same way about him. The miscarriage was simply too epic an event, a cut-off point between us, a brick wall that could never be breached. Our relationship was as dead as the short-lived pregnancy.

'Goodbye, Mike.' I said.

Shoulders slumped, Mike had gone on his way again, bewildered and confused. He seemed to have no clue what had happened, what he'd done wrong or why I was rejecting him. I felt sorry for him. Could he really have so little idea?

My mother appeared around the curtain the moment he was gone, all breezy smiles, packing my bag for me, trying to distract me. When she came to the flowers, she regarded them with a grim expression.

'What do you want me to do with these?' Mum said.

My first instinct was to throw them away. But on the same ward was an older lady. She was perhaps in her mid-forties, though her hair was thinning like an old man's and she seemed much older. She sat at the ward window all day in a large green chair. I wasn't sure what was wrong with her, though both her legs bandaged from ankle to knee. I'd tried to talk to her as I'd shuffled back from the toilet, but she'd merely glanced at me, a little irritated, before staring back again at the gargoyles that occupied the eaves of the building opposite. The only time she ever seemed to move was to get into bed at night. She had not had one single visitor in all the hours I was in hospital with her. I felt bad for her.

I picked up the flowers and approached the lady, who as usual had taken up her spot in the green chair next to the window. I held the flowers out to her, but she didn't appear to notice me.

I moved forwards, closer. 'Would you like these…?'

The lady looked at me. Her expression was vacant, almost like a small child's. Though she had seen me many times in the past few days, she regarded me as if she had first laid eyes on me. She said nothing.

'Please, have them.' I said.

The lady made no move to take them from me. Not sure what else to do, I stepped even closer and thrust the bouquet into her arms.

'Well, goodbye.' I said.

Still the lady said nothing. But she smiled.

I was discharged. Mum took me down to the car. Dad had taken the other girls back to the house in the hotel van. Getting in the car, I wanted to ask her so many things. *Had I done the right thing about Mike? How could I feel cheated and relieved at the same time about the pregnancy? Would I ever feel 'normal' again?* But I was so tired and I knew there would be more time for that later.

As Mum's little car travelled back towards home, I felt the tell-tale vibration of my mobile in my coat pocket. I hadn't looked at it since the night of the miscarriage. It had been left behind, plugged in at my dad's when he'd dashed me to the hospital. I slid the handset out of my pocket and looked at the screen, unsurprised at the number of notifications and icons. But before I could open or listen to any of them, the mobile rang in my hand.

'You going to get that?' Mum said, not taking her eyes off the road.

I looked back to the screen.

On it, a name blazed: SHONA ...

Shona

'My best friend is the person who, in wishing me well,
wishes it for my sake.'
Aristotle

Twenty-three

'… Hello?! Are you even listening to what I'm saying?'

The demand cut through the fog in my brain. For a moment, I had thought the words in my ear were one of my sister's … Amanda possibly, shaking me awake to tell me of her exploits the night before, unable to keep them to herself. But then I opened my eyes and I realised I was alone.

I was standing in those marketplace toilets again, the phone glued to my ear. The warm summer air felt stale. I caught sight of my reflection in the aluminium mirrors next to the hole-in-the-wall sinks, my expression impossible to read. At some point I must have kicked off one of my flip flops: the grimy tiles felt cold underneath my bare foot, the shoe nearby.

My bag lay on the counter, its contents spread everywhere. Lip gloss; a pocket dictionary; a half-eaten bag of crisps; a crumpled ball of receipts; various pens, most leaking; eyeliner; chewing gum; a cracked compact mirror; a box of tampons (*Won't be needing them…* a tiny voice in my head piped up). Finally, a notebook, two words written in capitals at a diagonal and underlined multiple times its message written ages ago yet fitting now: *OMFG*.

'Wait, what?' I said.

'Honestly Liz, you are unbelievable.' Shona said, with her habit of elongating any word with more than two syllables, always heavy on the stress: *unbellIEEEVable. ExCC-*

CEPTional. HilAAARious. I could see her in my mind's eye, sprawled on the bed in her Emo black and purple room, the blinds permanently drawn, rolling her eyes at me. 'Are we on for tonight or not?'

'Tonight?'

I tried gathering my thoughts, but every time I tried to focus, my brain came back empty. What were we doing tonight? I didn't care.

I stared at the pregnancy testing stick in my hand, the extra line that denoted the result: *positive*. Only that existed. It was not the first I had ever seen, but it had been the first that was mine. Before it had been Shona's, just a few months' earlier.

'I can't do it.'

Shona turned over and shoved the duvet over her head. She wouldn't even look at the kit I offered. I sighed. It had been up to me to buy it for her in the local pharmacy. I'd faced down the inquisitive looks with a nonchalant glare, hoping no one who knew me – or more importantly, Mum or one of my sisters – saw me.

'You have to.' I insisted.

Snorting and sighing like the teenage stereotype, Shona rose at last from her bed. She snatched the kit from my outstretched hand and swept into her en suite bathroom, slamming the door behind her. I heard the toilet seat lower. Then just as quickly, she was back at the bathroom door again.

'I can't go.' She announced.

I traipsed into the bathroom and turned the tap on. 'There.'

Shona just stood there. 'I'm not going in front of you.'

'You're not going at all. Apparently.' I countered.

A loaded – *pregnant?* – pause passed between us. I regarded my best friend, my arms folded, determined not to back down. I had never stood up to Shona before: always it was her lead, her ideas, her desires we followed. But the tables turned, just for a short while, as she and I faced up to each other.

Shona pursed her lips. 'Bobby Kingsmith.'

'That's who it was?' I said, unable to contain my surprise.

Of all the boys I had guessed Shona might have been with to prompt this pregnancy scare – and there were many - Bobby was not even on my radar. Bobby was a nerd. He was the type of guy who tucked his shirt into his jeans and brought sandwiches and a thermos flask to college. Bobby kept to himself, mostly sitting alone at college at lunch, even in class, guarding his work from prying eyes. He worked in the local hospital's radio station five nights a week, playing golden oldies for the Geriatrics ward. On Saturdays he could be found at school fetes and country fayres, covering them for the local paper. The eldest child of a single parent family, Bobby helped his mother out wherever he could: I'd seen him race off to do the weekly shop in-between college classes and he delivered his younger sister and brother to school in the mornings, so his mum could make it into work on time. Where could he have found time to squeeze sex with Shona into his busy schedule?

Shona's face crumpled. 'Yes.'

Suddenly, she was crying. I thought it was shame. I expected her to tell me she hadn't set out to have sex with Bobby. I waited for her to tell me she had been drunk: when wasn't she when chasing boys into bed? I even wondered if she would tell me it was a bet she hadn't felt she could lose face on or something equally far-fetched… Something simply more *Shona*. But she sat down on the bed with the still-unused pregnancy stick, her lip quivering.

'This will ruin everything for him.' She said.

My mind reeled. Shona actually cared what Bobby might think, or how an unplanned pregnancy might affect him?

'You… know him?' My brain reeled. This situation was

getting odder by the second.

Shona nodded, almost imperceptibly.

'When did this happen?'

'It was after Joe McIntosh's party.' Shona said in a small voice.

'Bobby wasn't at Joe's party.'

I didn't have to try and remember this fact. Bobby never went to parties. Bobby was always too busy (except when he wanted to have sex with Shona, apparently).

Shona sighed. 'I went to see him afterwards.'

'Why?' I was genuinely confused. '… How?'

The only time I had ever seen Shona interact with Bobby was on a maths project in Year Eight and she had sulked the entire time, speaking to him only when strictly necessary. Our teacher, Mrs. Moss had decided it would be 'just great' if everyone could partner with someone of the opposite sex. Of course, no one wanted to and so she'd forced us all. I'd got Simon Kitchen, a thin, willowy boy who won the four hundred metres every school sports day and smelled of the lemon fabric conditioner his mum used. I could remember little else about him, except the fact he died of Leukaemia in Year Ten. No one ever spoke about him after that, like we might die next if we did. Instead, there had been an assembly where the headmaster had talked in a low voice about the tragic Simon's 'passing' (he never used the word 'death'). Next had come a bench dedicated to Simon in the school quadrangle, the little brass plaque the only evidence he had ever been part of our lives.

'I got to know him, alright?' Shona said, defensive. 'I don't spend every waking moment with you, you know!'

Shona's words stung a little. 'You… love him?' The words felt strange, unwelcome in my mouth.

Shona grunted non-committally. 'Dunno.'

I felt betrayal pierce my heart. I had never had any real interest in Shona's boyfriends. Before now, she had always chosen walking clichés, the bad boys with piercings and tattoos and attitude problems. The kinds of guys who would have Shona in tears in the pub and nightclub toilets we'd managed to get in, underage. There, in-between sessions of drunken puking, I would hold her hair back as she urged and cried over the bowl. Poor messed-up Shona. Good old dependable Liz. It was the two roles we'd always played. Now here was good boy Bobby – *was he going to take my place?*

But Shona's pregnancy test – when she'd finally taken it hours later! - had come back negative.

Shona's relief had been huge, but mine even more so: had Shona been pregnant by Bobby Kingsmith, she would have been tied to someone other than me. Shona was the only person in my life I could call truly 'mine'. Friends since primary school, we'd shared everything: sleepovers, clothes, nights in and out, alcohol. I didn't have to share Shona with my sisters like I did my mother. My dad didn't belong to any of us. Mike, well … He was just Mike.

But Shona belonged to me.

Shona never mentioned Bobby again. I never knew if their relationship – if that's what it even was – continued, or if he was cast by the wayside, the latest in Shona's long line of conquests. I chose to believe the latter. For some reason though, I knew Bobby was different for her. The fact I had not been trusted with this information burned me up inside.

Looking at the positive pregnancy tester in my hand now, I felt a surge of resentment again. Shona got a 'near miss', yet here was I, pregnant? *It wasn't fair!*

Back in the toilets, at the end of the phone, Shona was talking again. 'I said we'd meet them at seven in The Moon.'

'Shut up.' I said suddenly, finding my voice from nowhere.

'What did you say?'

For a moment, I delighted in the shock in Shona's voice. Shona was the leader, she always had to be centre of attention: it was always about her, what she wanted. Well there were two people in this friendship and I was pretty sure my news would trump anything she had under her belt. *For once.*

'I'm pregnant.' I said.

Nothing. Whatever I expected from Shona now, it wasn't silence. But that's what I got.

'… Hello?' I said, thinking I might have been cut off.

'Yeah I'm here.' Shona said at last, in a curious flat voice. I waited another few moments as Shona picked her words. '… Herself's gone out. Come over here,' Shona instructed, 'we have to talk.'

'Herself' was Shona's mother and the least offensive of the names Shona called her. Some of the cleaner versions were 'Doormat' or 'Zombie'. In all the years I had known Shona, I realised I had no idea what her mum's actual name was. To me, she was always one of those names Shona called her, or perhaps Mrs. Talbot. Whatever her name, I realised with a jolt I'd never seen Shona's mum as a real person, but a kind of ghost, floating through Shona's house and our lives, barely making an impression. No wonder Shona's mum was so depressed: no one ever took any notice of her, not even long enough to learn her name.

'Ten minutes.' I said, hanging up.

Twenty-four

Shona's house was at the back of town. A real showpiece, it was part of a majestic red brick and sandstone estate on the clifftop. Each home was identical and haughty, like the cliques of girls at school who'd lounge on the low wall near the refectory. Those girls would never eat, but instead take tiny sips of bottled water to preserve their designer lip gloss, judging anyone who didn't look or even seem like them. I had badly wanted to be one of those perfect-seeming girls. I had wished initially I could live in a house like Shona's too, instead of the ramshackle, mouldy and occasionally flooded cottage I had grown up in. Yet as the years passed, I realised Shona's house was not a real home, just as I had seen the panic behind each of the cliquey girls' eyes at the thought of being found out as a fraud.

Shona came to the front door before I could even knock, spiriting me to her dingy bedroom. My earlier confession hung between us like the stale cigarette smoke inside. Several overflowing ashtrays balanced on books and shelves, in-between half-finished glasses of orange that smelled like vodka to my well-trained nostrils. I noted only some had Shona's blood-red lipstick around the rim. Had she had Bobby back here, smoking and drinking with her? I could imagine Bobby trying to impress her, coughing his lungs up and swaying round the room, unused to alcohol. He must have thought all his Christmases had come at once! *Beauty and The Geek*. I almost smiled at my ingenuity, before re-membering I had far more important things to worry about.

'What are you going to do?' Shona demanded, the mo-ment the bedroom door closed.

'I don't know.' I replied truthfully.

That loaded silence fell between us again, just like had done all those months ago when Shona had been in my place. Only it had worked out for her, hadn't it?

'Say you'd been pregnant...' I began.

'... I wasn't though, was I.' Shona deflected, as if even the thought could make it come true.

'Say you were.' I insisted. Shona rolled her eyes, as if she had been asked to do something particularly distasteful, like clean up dog sick. '... What would you have done?'

Shona opened a baccy tin and rolled a cigarette with one hand, licking the paper. For the first time, I wondered who had taught her to do that. Perhaps I had been wrong about Bobby. Could it have been him? Shona had only started smoking the last year or so, unlike most teens I knew who'd begun in Year Seven and already wanted to quit. I had not thought to ask why she had just started. *Shona was just... Shona.*

'I don't know!' Shona said.

Suddenly my resentment flared up again: Shona was the one with the secret boyfriend; Shona was the one who had got off the hook. I hadn't been so lucky. *She owed me!*

'Not good enough.' I stated, marvelling at the words coming out of me.

'What does that even mean?'

I'd heard Shona say that phrase to so many people: her parents, teachers, even people in the street. Usually it was a sarcastic retort to adults, an easy way of redirecting atten-tion back to her from discussion of politics, religion, even what was for dinner. She'd never said it to me before, but then I'd never given her cause to. Both of us squared up to each other, sure something had changed, but unsure what - besides the obvious.

'You and Bobby.' I said at last. 'You never told me.'

'There's nothing to tell.' Shona said automatically.

'I think there is.' I persisted.

'I'm not joking, don't go there Liz.' Shona said, her expression dark. 'What's this even got to do with anything?'

'I want to understand… Bobby Kingsmith? Seriously?'

'You don't know him.' Shona argued.

'I didn't even know you did!'

Another silence fell. Shona continued making cigarettes, dropping each ready-made into the baccy tin. I waited for her to say something. To tell me she loved Bobby; to tell me it had been a mistake – *anything!* Anything that would give me a clue. Because perhaps if I knew what Shona would have done had she been pregnant by Bobby, I would know now what to do next about my own predicament.

'I can't tell you what to do.' Shona said in a low voice, as if she had read my mind.

As soon as the words were spoken, I knew Shona was right. My chest suddenly felt tight as I faced up to the situation for the first time. I had been stalling, obsessing over Bobby and Shona in a bid to avoid making a choice myself.

I was pregnant. Me.

Only I could decide what to do next.

A deluge of emotions and thoughts overwhelmed me. I collapsed onto Shona's unmade bed, the tangle of sheets. Everything blurred together, a tidal wave of confusion, panic and fear. Tears made my vision blur, my shoulders wracked with sobs.

'… You're alright.' Shona soothed.

She sat next to me, her arm draped round my shoulders. I had a vague memory of sitting like this back in primary: I had skinned my knee. Shona had fetched a wet towel from the toilets and pressed it on the wound herself. She hadn't told the teacher. It was just me and her, just as it was now.

'How can this be alright?' I wailed.

Shona winced, as if expecting someone to come running from upstairs. No one did. When no one did, she said, 'You should tell Mike.'

'No.' I said, surprised at my own vehemence. 'You know what he's like.'

'So did you, but you still slept with him.'

Touché.

'He wouldn't be able to handle it…' I began.

'… Can you, on your own?'

I sighed. Shona had a point. Two people had created this pregnancy. Those same two people should be the ones to figure out what to do about it.

'Okay, let's tell him.' I said.

Twenty-five

Mike lived on the opposite side of town to Shona, about a twenty-five-minute walk away. Near the park, his terrace of houses had been the best town had to offer once, but their residents, with too much on and too little money, had let their homesteads fade. On the outside, Victorian bay windows fell victim to the weather; porches were covered in corrugated plastic; front gardens were paved over, weeds peeking up through the cracks. Inside, grimy net curtains flickered, the only sign of life from their mostly aged inhabitants.

As we approached the front door of Mike's place, I stopped. My heart was hammering, I struggled to catch my breath. Shona grabbed both my arms and made me look at her, making me think of primary again. But this time, for a moment I saw my mother in Shona's place: her comforting words on my first day at school, wiping my tears away. I had never thought of Shona as being maternal before now.

'Whatever happens, it'll be okay.' My best friend said.

Mute, I nodded. I knocked once, before letting myself in, just as I had always done. Shona stepped in after me. She had never actually been inside Mike's house before. Her nostrils flared in disgust. Though I had witnessed Francis push a vacuum around and wash up from time to time, he did little else by way of housework. Shelves were thick with dust, the mirror murky with grime. Tobacco fragments littered the carpet, clouds of dirt erupted from the sofa when it was sat on. Even the air felt old and dirty. Francis was a hoarder: stacks of newspapers and magazines occupied every available floor and counter space; dishes and mugs were left to gather mould; wrappers were left to crumple underfoot where they fell. The bathroom didn't even bear thinking about. The whole place was a health hazard.

'Francis?' I said.

I set one foot on the creaking stairs, Shona shuffling behind me. For the first time I noticed not only the dirt, but the neglected house underneath too: the faded and yellowed paintwork; the marks and gouges in the walls; the curling, stiff carpet. Mike's house was the exact opposite to Shona's, which was over-dressed, immaculate, magazine-inspired. Even so, each building had a lack of homeliness in common.

'He's upstairs.' Francis confirmed from the safety of the kitchen.

That room was a cocoon to him: an old man now, Francis had retired years ago. He didn't appear to have any friends or many visitors (unless you counted the milkman, who'd stop by for a chat every Tuesday. Who had milk delivered anymore?). Francis stood at the dirty kitchen countertop, turning the pages of his beloved newspapers and periodicals, listening to the radio and smoking his pipe.

When I'd started going out with Mike, I hadn't even known his father was home the first few times I had gone back to the house. Mike mentioned nothing and when our paths failed to cross those first few times, I just assumed Francis worked late or did night shifts. One night however, my hangover hit at three am and I crept down to the kitchen in my bra and knickers for a glass of water. Turning the kitchen overhead on, I discovered Francis had been seated at the kitchen table in the dark and I shrieked as if I had discovered a burglar.

'He doesn't sleep.' Mike said later, as if that explained

everything.

'He saw me in my underwear!' I raged.

'He's old.' Mike shrugged, 'Don't worry about it.'

Now, Shona and I climbed the narrow stairs up to Mike's attic bedroom. He was sprawled out on his grubby duvet in just his boxers, fiddling with a games console as various soldiers exploded and died on screen. He grinned as I came in, but his expression soon turned sour at the sight of Shona behind me.

'For God's sake Liz, you could've warned me, I'm half-dressed here.' Mike grumbled, pulling on a tee shirt he'd abandoned on the floor.

'Don't mind me.' Shona quipped, 'You haven't got anything I haven't seen before.'

'I bet.' Mike said.

'Funny you, aren't ya?' Shona smiled, but it didn't reach her eyes.

Mike and Shona couldn't stand each other. Mike had told me many times he thought her vain, egotistical and selfish. Shona had never said anything to me directly about Mike, but she'd made it plain she didn't like him with her usual rolled eyes every time I said his name. This was the first time they had been in the same room in nearly a year.

Shona plonked herself down on Mike's old futon, chucking various textbooks and detritus aside in a bid to make herself comfortable. She wanted a good seat for the show, no doubt. Even so, I was still glad I didn't have to face Mike on my own.

'So, what do you girls want?' Mike said.

You girls. If I ever chose to involve anyone in my life but Mike, it seemed I was on the opposite 'side' to him.

'We were… I was just…' My eyes darted to Shona, who nodded to me as if to say *Go on.* '… I've got something to tell you.'

Mike folded his arms and waited for the revelation. He

knew that whatever I had to say, it wasn't good.

'I'm pregnant.' I said.

Shona looked like she might explode with anticipation of Mike's reaction. I could see her hand hovering in her pocket. I thought she would film him, stick it on YouTube. Later she would tell me she had the police on speed dial, 'just in case'.

'There's two potentially dangerous times in a pregnant woman's life.' She said, 'When she actually has the baby – obviously – and when she tells the father.'

'That's ridiculous.' I scoffed.

'It's true!' Shona said, her expression earnest, 'I saw it on the True Crime channel.'

'Oh, must be true then.' I said, rolling my own eyes at her.

Now, I was not so sure. There was barely a ripple of movement in Mike's features, but I could tell how angry he was. There was a dark fury to him, seething underneath. A part of me wanted to explode with apologies and explanations, to try and make the situation right again. But another look from Shona silenced me before I could even begin: *Don't you dare.*

'And it's mine?' Mike said at last. He fished a half-smoked cigarette from an overflowing ashtray and lit it, grimacing at the taste of relit tobacco.

'… What? There's only ever been you.' I whispered.

If Mike heard me, he pretended he didn't. 'I wouldn't ask,' Mike said complacently, taking another drag: 'Except, well … You do hang around with *her*.'

He raised an eyebrow at Shona as he said this. Suddenly Shona was on her feet. She grabbed at Mike's tee shirt as if attempting to shake some sense into him. Mike only raised one hand to push her away, but Shona almost fell backwards. She cartwheeled her arms in an attempt to stay upright, before grabbing the wall to save herself.

'Oh classy.' Shona spat, massaging her shoulder. She was wearing a vest top. I could see the flesh was red, where it had hit the brick of the attic wall. A nasty bruise would form there tomorrow. 'Manhandling a girl. Nice one, Keegan!'

'Don't bother playing the girl card.' Mike drawled, bored. 'You came at me, remember? If you're gonna play feminists, at least practice what you preach.'

'You're unbelievable,' Shona breathed, her voice dangerously low.

I stood between them before the fight could get more physical.

'Don't!' I turned to Shona, 'Could you... Wait downstairs? *Please.*'

Behind me, I knew Mike would be eyeballing my best friend with a sarcastic grin. It was about winning and losing with him, so he'd figure I was on his side for sending her downstairs. I squeezed her arm to say 'sorry'.

Shona sighed and backed down. Still looking at Mike, she said to me, 'I'll be in the kitchen. Alright?'

The subtext was clear: if Shona heard too much or Mike got physical with me, she'd spill her guts to Francis. I loved her for that, especially as Mike appeared to shrink under the weight of the threat.

'Later.' She said to Mike.

Mike made a face at her, mimicked her under his breath like a child. *What had I ever seen in him?* As soon as the attic door swung behind her, Mike was his usual self, all swagger and bravado in the safety of his room.

'So?' He said.

'So. It's yours.' I confirmed, pushing down my anger. I needed to keep a clear head, however ugly this got.

'Do you want money, is that it?'

For a moment I thought he meant a payoff. Yet I was no shark-like groupie and Mike was no celebrity, however high on himself he was. He had no public good name, nor was he married with an existing wife to lose. More importantly, he had no wealth. *What the hell was he on about?*

Mike raised his eyes skywards, realising I was not catching on. 'For the abortion?'

The abortion. As if that was the only option. Not 'an abortion', as one of many things to be explored. Mike's mind was already made up: there could be only one outcome here.

'I don't know if that's what I want.' I said.

'And what about what I want?'

'We need to decide what happens next.' I pleaded, 'I just want to look at all the options …?'

'… Sounds like you've made your mind up already.'

'Yeah? Ditto!' I countered.

Stalemate. The weight of the situation between us, Mike and I stared at each other, both of us searching for words. I found myself staring at the hairs on his arms, the veins bulging in his skin, his anger and frustration – and fear? - Clear. His cigarette dangled from his slack hand, forgotten. The end had fallen off: more ash upon the filthy carpet, the burning ember making a hot rock in the fibres. Mike did not notice or care.

'I'm the one who's pregnant.' I pointed out. 'If you don't want to be involved ...?'

'… Except I am involved!' Mike interjected, raising his voice at last. He couldn't even so much as let me finish my sentence. 'Even if I walk away, there'd still be a kid somewhere in the world, related to me whether I like it or not! How'd you think that makes me feel?'

'Well you should have thought of that, then!' I spat back at him.

I couldn't believe it. Mike would rather simply erase all evidence of the pregnancy, rather than discuss it, like an adult. Yet standing before me in a tee shirt and boxers, his pale stick-like legs on display, his eyes shining with frustrated tears, I suddenly realised: Mike was just a boy.

What was I – a girl? Or a woman?

'I don't want a kid.' Mike said at last. His tone made me think of a child caught in the throes of a tantrum, telling his mother he didn't want dinner, or to put his clothes on. Not something as epic as this.

'I don't know if I want one, either…' I began.

'… Well, then!' Mike interrupted. Another of his stock phrases. Along with 'So?', these two sentences formed the basis of most of his arguments.

I grit my teeth. 'I just want to talk about this. Properly.'

'What is there to talk about?' Mike said.

'Everything…!'

'… No.'

There it was: an end to the matter. Mike did not want to discuss anything with me. Mike was only interested in one way of resolving the situation: *his* way. As far as he was concerned, if I wanted my feelings taken into account too, then I was the one being unreasonable.

'You're unbelievable.' I said, echoing Shona earlier.

Mike shrugged and stubbed out his long dead cigarette at last. 'I'm going to university in a couple of weeks.'

'So am I.' I said, baffled.

'Good luck with that.' Mike asserted. 'On your own, a kid, rent to pay, studies to do… Yeah, hope it works out for you. Truly.'

His words didn't make sense at first. Then with sickening clarity, they hit me. He was washing his hands of me. He didn't care what I did about the pregnancy, as long as I did it as far away from him as possible.

I was well and truly dumped.

'You bastard.' Venom flooded through my words, my body. I didn't believe I could hate anyone more than I did Mike in that single moment.

'Just… go, will you?' Mike said. 'You're embarrassing

yourself.'

I just stood there. Mike began the computer game again: gunfire sounded again around the attic bedroom. I stared at the back of his head, willed him to turn around. To look at me, realise his mistake, or at least the vile way he was treating me. *What was wrong with him?*

But he didn't.

'Goodbye, then.' I said.

Mike gaze was still fixed on the computer game and the carnage on-screen. My legs felt heavy. I shuffled my way from the bedroom, sure he would call after me.

But he didn't.

Shona was waiting for me at the bottom of the stairs. 'I tell you, if that guy smells even half as bad as this house, I'm not going near him,' Shona chortled in her too-loud voice.

I knew Francis must be able to hear her, but I just didn't care. For once, Shona's rudeness was the least of my problems.

'So, what did the runt say?'

Shona always called Mike 'the runt': unlike many of our male friends, Mike was short, perhaps five seven, though he always insisted he was five ten. Yet that would have made him at least as tall as Hannah, who outstripped him by miles.

'He…' I felt hot tears prick my eyelids, a lump rose in my throat. 'He, um …?'

I didn't need to say it.

Shona's face became dark as thunder. '… Arsehole!'

She moved towards the stairs again. She was going up to confront him.

I stood in her way. 'Don't. It'll only make things worse.'

'How can it be worse!' Shona shrieked.

She was right; it couldn't be any worse. But even so, I wanted to walk out the front door with some dignity. Shona rolled her eyes at me; it was clear she thought I was weak. Shona took my arm, propelled me towards the front door.

'Let's go, then.' She said grimly.

Twenty-six

As soon as Francis' front door slammed after us, the tears started. For a few moments there were hysterical gulps of air and snot as panic hit me. *What the hell was I going to do?* My shoulders wracked with sobs, Shona just gave me a hankie. She guided me down the back roads, away from the park and the high street and other people.

I didn't ask where we were going. Shona dragged me back to her parents' home, through the front door. There, in the hallway, was a huge ornate mirror next to the phone. As we crossed the threshold, she pointed at it, made me look at my reflection. In the glass, my face was crumpled and red, my mascara and eye shadow smeared. I looked a mess. And very, very young.

'Remember this.' Shona instructed.

I wondered what Shona meant. Before I could ask, her attentions were diverted. She grabbed at the many coats on the hook. She felt in the pockets, swearing when she didn't find what she needed.

'Dad …? Dad!' She bellowed. 'Borrowing the car.'

It was a scene I'd witnessed countless times before. Shona never asked for anything, yet always got what she wanted.

'Keys on the hook, darling.' Philip, her father, called from the kitchen. He didn't even come through and ask where we were going.

The car keys were right in front of her, on the hook above the telephone as Philip promised. Shona cast a sneaky look back towards the kitchen, then opened the telephone table drawer. Inside was a very expensive calfskin wallet: Phillip's. She checked the cash inside and sighed. Only twenty pounds.

'Typical,' Shona hissed, 'He always has at least three hundred, four hundred in here. But not today!'

'What do you want it for?' I said, wide-eyed.

But Shona ignored me. She drew out a credit card, then searched through the rest of the wallet. She produced a scrap of paper, with a number on it: Philip's PIN.

'Well done Dad, always security conscious.' The sarcasm dropped off Shona like raindrops.

She led me through the hall inner door to their massive garage. Inside, were two of their cars, the third presumably still out with Shona's mother. I knew Shona wasn't supposed to drive Phillip's Jaguar, but she unlocked it and slid in behind the steering wheel.

'Get in.' She told me.

'Where are we going?'

All my previous fight had left me. Now I just wanted everything back to normal. First stop: Shona telling me what to do.

'To get this sorted.' Shona tapped something into the very expensive car's satnav. It was like the dashboard to launch a spaceship.

Forty or so minutes through country roads and three run red lights later, Shona pulled up on a side street on a double yellow line. I recognised where we were, if not the actual road. She'd taken me inland, to Exmorton. We were outside a large Victorian house with lots of hanging baskets and a brass bell, though there was a modern intercom system as well. A large, newly-painted sign proclaimed: 'The Stevenson Well Woman Clinic.' A couple of women and a man stood nearby, with clipboards, a megaphone and a sign that read: FOETUSES ARE PEOPLE TOO, with a very badly drawn baby underneath. Protestors. They were taking a break, lolling against a well-pruned hedge.

I knew why Shona had brought me to this place. 'An abortion clinic?'

Shona shrugged. 'I didn't know what else to do. Do you?'

'I don't have any money…' I began, then quieted as Shona flicked her father's credit card at me. So that's what it was for. 'But I can't afford to pay him back … He'll miss it?'

'No, he won't.' Shona replied with undisguised bitterness, not meant for me.

We sat for some moments in the car, in silence. I took in the big white building and its ridiculously jolly flower arrangements. I wasn't sure how I felt about being there. I could walk in there with Shona's dad's credit card and this walking nightmare of an afternoon would be over in just a few hours. Or I could turn away and figure out another way … Whatever that was.

Finally, Shona broke the silence. 'Do you want to go inside?'

'I don't know.' I confessed.

Shona sighed, tried another tack. 'Okay. Do you want this baby?'

Baby. I'd been trying to keep that word out of my mind, referring to it as 'the pregnancy' instead. Babies had always been positive things to me and my family, something to be celebrated. I remembered going to the hospital with my mother, seeing the twins on the fuzzy black and white screen, my mother's happy tears. There had never been twins in either side of the family before.

But at the same time, the word 'baby' to me now inspired a feeling of trepidation within me. Babies meant change and

I had things I wanted to do. But …

'… I don't know!'

Shona drummed her fingers on the steering wheel, her irritation with me rising. She had a final go at coaxing an answer from me:

'Do you want an abortion?'

'No.'

The word seemed to jump out of me, by itself. *Where had that come from?* I guessed it had been there all along, in the back of my mind. Mike had been right.

'Looks like you're having a baby, then.' Shona said.

I felt sick. I undid my seatbelt and lurched out the car door. I clambered out of the car, towards the drain by the double yellows. All I managed was a couple of dry heaves. Shona followed me, leaving the car engine running.

'You're alright.' She said. Again.

Except I wasn't. I was miles from alright. I might have made some kind of decision – *I didn't want an abortion* – but still I was struck by fear and dread. Did all mothers-to-be feel like this? I doubted it. My mother had always been so happy to discover she was expecting, even though Dad flitted in and out of our lives. Mum was built for all this. I was not.

'Are you okay, love?'

It was a woman's voice. Shona and I looked up to see one of the protestors had broken away from her small group. She was a dumpy young woman with a long, balding green corduroy coat and a wicker hat jammed over most of her face. A cruel part of me wondered if she had ever had a lover; I bet she'd never had to deal with unexpected pregnancy. Then I remembered Shona and Bobby: there was someone for everyone. Except me, it seemed.

'She's fine.' Shona said, her tone brittle, eager to get away. I knew how she felt about such people. She'd joined Twitter just to troll religious people; there wasn't any other reason for being on there, as far as she was concerned.

'I was talking to your friend.'

The woman in green ignored Shona, despite my friend's best efforts to jam me back in the car. In the woman's hand, a selection of pamphlets. She offered me one. I reached out to take it. I looked at the leaflet the woman had given me. Across the top the words, 'ADOPTION – A REAL CHOICE' were emblazoned.

Shona got in the way. 'Look, you don't need to convert anyone here, okay?'

'That's not what I'm trying to do.' The woman said quietly. She rejoined her group of friends outside the clinic doors.

'Do-gooding nutcase.' Shona proclaimed after her. *There was the Shona I knew.*

'Take me home.' I whispered.

Silence descended between us as Shona drove. Halfway home, Shona flicked on the radio. The car was filled with jaunty pop tunes about relationships and sex. Stories of how much fun men and women could have; how nothing stands in the way of a boy and girl in love. I had believed them once upon a time, just as I had believed Mike and I had something … If not love, then at least some sort of friendship. Now I realised, too late, we'd had nothing.

I stared at the leaflet in my hand all the way. On the front were pictures of babies, smiling adults. 'Give the gift of life to someone who can't have their own child' the pamphlet's caption suggested.

There must be hundreds of real adults in the world who could give my child the type of home I never could? Faint optimism gripped me as I thought it over. I could still have the life I was meant to, the child could still have theirs. The more I read the black type, the more I believed it could be a possible solution.

Shona stopped at the top of the lane like she always did,

so I might cut across the field to my house. A hand-painted sign protruding from the hedge promised cream teas in the village; another grammatically incorrect board invited people to 'pick their own strawberry's.' Shona turned the engine off; the radio abruptly died. Silence filled up the space between us.

'Tell your Mum.' She said softly.

'I can't.'

'For God's sake, Liz!' Shona exploded, 'If anyone will understand, it's her. She's had literally half a dozen babies herself!'

'Exactly!' I argued. 'She's got too much on.'

'Not for you.' Shona said vehemently.

'You don't get it. I'm the good one!'

All my life, I had been the 'helper'. I had always been the one who could be counted on not to tantrum, to help tidy up, to help keep the other kids in line when my father had gone AWOL. I wasn't so much as a daughter, as back-up. I could remember Mum's words as far back as a small girl of four or five: *What a good girl you are. You're such a help to Mummy. What would I do without you?*

'Tell. Her.'

'I can't.' I repeated, my eye drawn back to the leaflet.

Shona's gaze followed mine, my train of thought. 'You're not …?'

'… Why not?'

'Adoption??'

'Adoption is a good thing.' I pointed out.

'Yes,' Shona agreed. 'It is. For orphans … And for children whose parents can't cope, or never wanted them in the first place.'

'Like me, you mean.'

'No.' Shona shook her head, like she knew what was best for me. 'This isn't you, Liz. I know it's not what you expected, but you'd be alright …!'

'… You don't know that.'

'You'd have to go through the entire pregnancy … The birth… And then stand back and watch a stranger take your baby away! This is not an easy option.'

'I never said it was.' I shot back.

'This isn't a soap opera, Liz!' Shona said, exasperated.

La la la … I wasn't listening. I had turned into Mike. I stuck with it. 'It would be for the best.'

'For whom…?'

'For both of us.'

Shona actually laughed. 'You don't know what you're talking about.'

'And you do?'

'No,' Shona admitted. 'But I know someone who does.'

With that, Shona turned the key in the ignition and the engine fired back into life.

Twenty-seven

'What are you doing, Shona!'

The car's wheels spun around. Shona stuck the car in reverse, almost crashing back into the field's small stone wall behind us. She turned the wheel again, yanking it and suddenly we were travelling the way we'd come, back towards Exmorton.

In the rear-view mirror, Shona's expression was crazed. My phone buzzed in my pocket. I took it out and saw Mum's name on the screen: *YOU SHOULD HAVE BEEN HOME HOURS AGO,* her text read. Great, now I was for it. But I had Shona to deal with first. I tapped out a reply: *SORRY, HOME SOON.* But would I? I had no idea, with Shona being so weird.

'Where are we going this time?' I asked, for the hundredth time.

'You'll see.' Shona said through clenched teeth.

We made it into Exmorton, pulling up outside another Victorian house. This one was grander than the abortion clinic. No expense had been spared. Beautiful topiary in the shapes of birds and animals surrounded the whitewashed building; velvet curtains were visible through the French windows. Elderly residents played bowls on the lush green grass, or sat out under huge parasols, chatting amongst themselves. The occasional white-clad staff member was visible amongst them, talking softly or playing cards. An old people's home. A very expensive one at that.

'Why are we here?'

Again, Shona did not answer my question. She got out of the car and waited on the gravel pathway: she expected me to do the same. I sighed, undid my seatbelt and followed her.

Shona went into the building. I hung back, looking around me. Unlike the outside, the interior was more recognisable: despite the chandeliers, there was a medicinal-like smell, a patterned carpet. It was half-hospital, half-hotel. I had a vague memory of visiting my grandfather, my father's father, in a place like this years ago. It has been an NHS hospital, with a floor so shiny, so your shoes squeaked on it. Amanda, Sal and I had spent the afternoon sliding up and down the corridor while Dad said goodbye to an unconscious man in an oxygen mask.

'You were never there for me.'

I heard Dad's words as I slid past on my knees, almost crashing into a trolley of covered meals coming the other way. Mum appeared as if from nowhere, lips pursed. She did not say anything. She grabbed my arm and pulled me after her, instructing Sal and Amanda to fall into line, follow her. After that, we waited in the car after that until Dad reappeared. His eyes were shining and there was one of those false smiles painted on his face.

'I'm fine.' He said as my mother drove away (he was not fine).

'He was your father.' Mum said in a low voice we weren't meant to hear.

'No.' Dad said, 'He was just a man.'

Ahead of me, Shona disappeared into a room. Number seventy-eight. On the door was a selection of pictures, ranging from kids' pics of paint and potato print through to computer graphics. For some reason, I knew Shona had done every single one. Whomever was inside this room had been there a long time. Who was it?

I took a deep breath and pushed the door open. The room was pleasant; it might have been a swanky bed and breakfast if you didn't know. Shona was fussing around with various things. She took dead flowers from a vase; rearranged magazines; remade the bed, even though it didn't need doing. Shona's busy-ness felt forced, like she was trying to distract herself.

A woman was seated in a well-padded chair at the window. Though she had silver hair plaited loosely down her back, she was not as old as I expected: perhaps fifty-five. Her face was lined, severe, no make-up. She wore old lady's clothes: pearls, a twin set, box-pleated skirt. On her feet were bright cerise slippers, trimmed with fake fur. The contrast was ridiculous, yet the slippers seemed familiar. A moment later, I realised where I had seen them before: on Shona. I looked up, to find Shona's gaze on me.

'This is my aunt.' Shona explained. 'My father's older sister, Natalie.'

In all the years I had known her, Shona had never mentioned she had an aunt. I had a thousand questions, the most pressing being why she had brought me here. Instead I said:

'Hello, Natalie.'

Natalie looked at me as if she had seen me for the first time. 'Hello, dear.'

I could tell, somehow by instinct alone, Natalie was not in the home because she was old. There was nothing in the way she held herself that said she was disabled, had suffered a stroke, or had dementia, either. It was her eyes that gave it away. Natalie stared into the distance at something so far away, it was as if she could never join us back in reality. Wherever she was, her sad expression told me her world was full of pain.

Shona gulped. She did not want to say what she was about to, but something about my friend's own expression told me she felt she had to:

'Tell her about Toby.' Shona said.

Natalie's agonised features moved. A mother's indulgent smile appeared at her lips, lighting up her face.

'He was a lovely baby,' she said, picking an imaginary piece of lint off her tweedy, old lady skirt. 'Full head of hair when he was born. Jet black. Beautiful big eyes.'

Shona had heard this story many times before, I could tell. I saw her lips form Natalie's words silently as her aunt said them.

'Where is he, now?' Shona prompted, almost cringing. It was clear she hated what she was doing. Yet I felt power-less to watch and listen, in that disinfectant-smelling, hos-pital-like room.

'Mum said it was for the best.'

Something about Natalie's voice, face, changed as she said this. The older woman appeared to shrink in her chair, her posture child-like. But what was worse: that age-old agony appeared on her features again, pain as clear at the memory as if the event had happened yesterday.

'What happened, Natalie?' Shona said softly.

'Mum said it wasn't right, a young girl having a baby out of wedlock.' Natalie whispered, 'People would reckon I was wicked. I'd never get a good job, never get married. No money. No money, no baby. It's for the best.'

For the best... What I had said to Shona earlier.

Horror flooded through me. I'd read on the internet about young girls being pressurised to give their babies up for adoption by parents and even the government, but I'd never met a woman who had been forced to make such a choice. My heart ached for Natalie.

But most of all, I was angry. With Shona. *How could she emotionally blackmail like me like this?*

'Stop it.' I said darkly.

Shona shot me a look. 'Did he ever come and find you?'

Natalie shook her head. A single tear escaping the corner of her left eye, tracking its way down her over-rouged cheek. 'I put my name on all the lists.' She said, 'I always hoped. But … nothing.'

'That's enough.' A lump rose in my throat. I didn't want to hear anymore. I didn't know if I could.

'Natalie tried to get on with her life,' Shona said to me, 'But it always came to back to this … Wondering about him. Is he happy? Sad? Alive… dead?'

'I said stop it.'

'You need to know,' Shona said. 'If you're going to live with it?'

'Stop it!'

Something snapped. I bolted. Out of that hospital-like room, away from poor, lost Natalie. Down the corridor, dodging trolleys and residents, out into the open air of the driveway beyond.

Twenty-eight

I emerged into the summer evening. Passing from the stuffy corridor into the colder air beyond, I shivered. The dark night touched my arms, making the fine hairs there stand up. My heart was hammering. I struggled to swallow, a ball of pain caught in my throat.

Shona was wrong to bring me to see Natalie. If I put *my* baby up for adoption? It would be *my* choice. No one was forcing me, like Natalie's mother had forced her. I wasn't stupid either. I knew it was a huge thing to do. It was me who would have to carry the baby; I would have to give birth. And yes, I would be the one who would have to hand the child over. But I could do it: I was being responsible! It was the best thing for everyone.

Why couldn't Shona see that?

I saw the sun dipping over the horizon ahead and realised the last buses of the day must have finished. Irritated, I stood next to the car and waited for Shona. She must have known I was going nowhere, because she sidled out of the home about twenty minutes later, unlocking the Jaguar with the remote fob. She slid in behind the wheel without looking at me.

She reached over, opening the passenger side door for me. 'Are you getting in, then?'

I sat down, slamming the car door. Shona didn't react.

'That was a low trick.'

'Not a trick.' Shona said, 'Did you see her face? You think I liked putting her through that?'

'You just have to be right, don't you?'

'It's not about being right!'

Finally, a real reaction from Shona. She slammed a hand on the steering wheel. Her eyes shone with tears, her face flushed red.

'For God's sake Liz! This about you. And that baby!'

An uneasy silence settled on the car.

'Adoption's not wrong.' I said at last.

Shona sighed, pinching her nose with her thumb and forefinger as if warding off a headache – or perhaps counting to ten. 'Of course it isn't. But it is for you.'

'How do you know?' I demanded.

'Because I know you.'

I sighed. I was unsure what Shona was seeing that I couldn't. I wasn't ready to be a mother. No matter what Shona said or thought, that wouldn't suddenly change. But I didn't want to have an abortion. What else was there to do? Adoption was the obvious answer: I could still have my life, the child too. It was sensible, responsible. Okay, it would be hard, but then things worth doing often were. My own mother had taught me that.

Shona started the engine and we were on the road again. Night fell and the lights of Exmorton fell to the darkness of the countryside. Other cars' headlights and the cat's eyes on the road flashed by.

In my pocket, my mobile vibrated with half a dozen notifications. Mum had enlisted my sisters' help in tracking me down: a Snapchat message from Amanda showed a picture of my sister making a face with the words: YOU IN TRUB-BLE NOW in illuminous letters. I knew she was right but did not reply.

I was so confused. If Shona was not trying to emotional-ly blackmail me in doing what *she* believed was right – keep the baby – then what was she doing?

'I thought you didn't like children?'

Shona never took her eyes off the road. 'I don't.'

'You took me to an abortion clinic!' I pointed out.

'I know.' She said.

'Then why are you bothered if I keep it or not?'

We completed the rest of the journey in silence. Shona stopped at the top of the lane again, just as she had earlier, in daylight. The darkness swallowed up those handmade signs; the field I usually cut across was a yawning mouth beyond the hedge. When the car came to a standstill, I muttered my thanks and grabbed for the door handle. I just wanted to get out of the vehicle and away from Shona, the weirdness between us.

'Liz.'

I looked back, still angry with my best friend. But Shona started ahead, through out of the windscreen, as if she didn't trust herself to look directly at me.

'You have everything I ever wanted. You know that?'

Confusion whirled through my head for the millionth time that day. Shona was crazy. What the hell did I have, that she could want? I was pregnant, with no boyfriend, no money, my whole future hanging in the balance! But I was too tired to argue with her anymore.

''Bye, Shona.' I let the car door click shut.

Shona turned her head and gave me one last look up and down, as if committing me to memory. The car engine turned over. With another spin of wheels in the country mud, my best friend was gone.

Twenty-nine

It was a humid, August night. In the dark out here, I might be the only person in the world: it certainly felt like it. In the woods I could hear a fox barking. Heavy machinery chugged somewhere out in the fields or up on the main road, working late. A light breeze whispered through the boughs of the trees that created a canopy of leaves over the road. The pale eye of the moon poked through, high in the sky. An apocalypse could happen away in the towns and cities, but out in the sticks, our lives would remain undisturbed, forgotten.

I managed to find the stile that led into the field beyond the lane. I climbed it, swinging my legs over. I caught my rucksack's strap on the barbed wire on the fence next to it. Swearing, I pulled it free. I ignored the sound of ripping fabric, hoping it wasn't as bad as it sounded. There were no other houses on the lane and I could see just one light on in the valley below: my house. Within, my mother would be waiting up for me.

My heart sank, though I'd known this would happen. I also knew, once in the house, I would have to explain myself by telling my mother what had happened that day. She would never let it go otherwise. We would be there all night – what was left of it – if necessary. I could already hear her voice, ringing in my ears: *where have you been? Why haven't you answered your phone? I've been worried sick!*

I gritted my teeth. So many people, all going on at me. First Mike's accusations; then Shona emotionally blackmailing me or God-knows-whatever she was doing. I wasn't sure I could take Mum as well.

You have everything I ever wanted.

I stopped in the long grass. Realisation hit me with the force of iced water. Shona hadn't been talking about my situation. She hadn't meant the pregnancy, Mike, or the choice I would have to make.

She was talking about Mum.

'Tell your Mum.' She'd said in the car.

'She's got too much on.' I'd protested.

'Not for you.'

All my life I had guarded my friendship with Shona from my family jealously, keeping her away from my sisters rather than share her. I had forced Shona to stay on the fringe of my life. That suited me, but not her. It was the same with her parents. Her father was always away on too-frequent business trips; her mother in a drug-induced haze. Yet despite having never had one in her life, she could recognise a dependable person – my Mum.

Mothers in the past may not have been supportive of their pregnant underage daughters, but even if they had wanted to, society would not have let them. But it was different now. As I had insisted in the car, adoption could be a good thing. These days, no one could force a young single mother into having her baby taken away if she wanted to keep it. Somehow, Shona had known before I had.

I wanted the baby!

Shona had looked into my soul and seen that for all my bluster about being sensible and responsible, a part of me deep down ached at the thought of giving my child away. That was why Shona had taken me to see Natalie: not to scare me into agreeing with her, but to show me the consequences of going against my instinct.

Remember this, Shona had instructed in the hallway as I'd looked at my reflection, young and defeated, in the mirror. I had wondered what to do next, but I now realised Shona had told me that moment had to be my starting point, where I began. There was no further down for me; I had hit rock bottom. The only way was up, whatever my decision was.

I didn't have to do it alone.

I wasn't sure exactly why I wanted the baby; it just seemed… *right*. Shona had reached out to me in my confusion and reminded me there were people in my life who could help me. I had thought Shona had somehow 'owed' me, back in her bedroom; but really it was me who owed her.

And I had rejected her.

I grabbed for my phone in my pocket, intent on calling my best friend. I wanted to make Shona turn the car around, come back up the country lane so I could throw my arms around her and tell her I was sorry. Sorry for rejecting her; sorry for side-lining her; sorry for not getting what she was trying to do for me. I wanted to say I understood now: adoption was wrong for me, but more than that, it was wrong for the rest of my family, too. My family, for all its problems, would welcome another child, even one conceived in less than ideal circumstances. My mother would want to help me; my sisters would want their first niece or nephew kept in the family. We could figure out the rest later.

But before I could select Shona's number from my contact list, my phone lit up in my hand. It started to ring, its harsh tone sounding even louder in the middle of the dark field. Surprised, I peered at the screen.

On it, my little sister's name, SAL…

All of them

'Don't think, or judge. Just listen.'
Sarah Dessen

Thirty

'Don't say anything, okay?'

The room shimmered into focus, the words booming in my ears. I was startled to realise they were coming from my own mouth. My vision was threatened by blue tinges, like I might pass out. I felt like I had just woken up, limbs heavy and sluggish. I jumped at the sound of my voice: it seemed to rumble around the grotty toilets and echo back at me, like I was in a cave.

'You don't even know why I'm calling!' Sal said, 'I wanted…'

I interrupted her. '… I need to talk to Mum.'

'So, call her!' Sal's tone was more bewildered than annoyed now. She'd never heard me talk to her like this before.

'I'm pregnant.' I said.

There was silence at the end of the line.

'Are you sure?' Sal said at last.

I looked at the pregnancy tester in my hand, just to make sure it wasn't all some freaky dream. The two crossed lines were proof enough.

'Yup.'

'Get rid of it.' Sal said.

'What?' My mind was reeling. 'Just get Mum …!'

'Get rid of it, or you'll be ruining your life.'

'I don't know what I want to do yet!' I tried to point out,

'This is why I need to speak to Mum!'

'You know what she's like! It's babies, babies, babies with her!' Sal kept her voice down. On the other end of the phone, I heard a door close. She was hiding away somewhere, trying to get me to see sense.

I clenched my fists. 'I told you: I don't know what I want to do yet.'

'Mum will make you keep it.' Sal said.

I couldn't believe it. Did my sister really just see our mother as some kind of baby-maker? She was so much more than that. Sure, Mum was annoying, even scary at times: she could snap as easily as a dry twig. I hated Mum sometimes, but I admired her all of the time. She was hardworking, always. She was always there for us. Why couldn't Sal see that?

I took a deep breath. 'Please get Mum.'

I heard Sal swear at the end of the line. Then there was the sound of a door opening and the rustling of a phone on the move. I heard the tinny radio in the kitchen, playing Mum's beloved Euro Pop. Sal muttered something. There was more rustling and then suddenly Mum's voice filtered through

'Hello darling,' Mum said, her tone light and breezy. 'Where are you? I'm making your favourite for dinner.'

My favourite: lasagne, then. The change in tack of conversation, from the monumental to the every-day, brought a lump to my throat and the sting of tears to my eyes.

'Great,' I gulped, the air seeming to press on my chest. 'Mum, I need to talk to you.'

Mum's initial breeziness was gone in an instant. 'What's the matter, Lizzie? Are you alright?'

'Yes.' I said immediately, then changed my mind. '…No. Can you come and get me?'

Within moments, the lasagne duties had been abandoned to a grumbling Sal. Mum dropped everything to come and fetch me as I'd asked. She told me not to worry and she'd be with me soon.

I left the toilets and real life resumed once again. I noticed the lack of stalls; over half the pitches were empty, despite the midday sun being high in the sky. It was matched by the lack of customers. There was just a handful of old people drifting here and there, examining products and tat with eyes and hands. I must have been the youngest in the market place by about forty years.

I wandered stall to stall with unseeing eyes, trying to keep busy but really just going over the same question in my mind: *how was I going to break this news to Mum, where did I even begin?*

Then there was the beep of a horn in the car park beyond the marketplace. Mum wasn't supposed to park there when the market was on, but she'd never cared for rules of the road. As Dad always said, Mum saw the amber light as a challenge. She had a glove compartment full of parking tickets all year round. Twice she had run over pheasants and then brought them back to the house to eat (though she'd not told us until after the meal). Now Hannah and Sal refused to touch poultry at all, until Mum assured them it was not roadkill.

I trudged over to Mum's little car. I wrenched open the car door and sat down in the passenger seat. She was silent, her face impassive, giving nothing away. The radio was not on. The air felt heavy as she waited for me to begin.

'I'm pregnant.' I said at last, taking the plunge.

'I know, Sal said before I left.'

Typical Mum. A flash of irritation burst through me: couldn't she have spared me my confession? But I knew she couldn't.

'Are you angry?'

'Angry?' Mum seemed genuinely surprised. 'No. Worried for you? Yes.'

There was a pause as I drank this in. I had expected even just a half-raised voice, or expression of disappointment. Yet Mum seemed to mean it.

'I don't know what to do.'

'You're a bright girl, Lizzie.' Mum chastised. 'You know what options are available. What you mean is, you can't decide.'

'It has to be my decision.' I said, remembering Sal's assertion on the phone. I didn't truly believe my little sister could be right, but I had to be sure. I needed Mum to know I would be doing what I wanted, not what she wanted.

'Of course.' Mum's tone was incredulous, as if she wouldn't even entertain me doing otherwise. I smiled, relieved, feeling hopeful for the first time in an hour – until she followed up with:

'Shall we go and see your father?'

I nodded and Mum started the car again.

Thirty-one

We zoomed over to The Belle View Hotel, the latest place unfortunate enough to employ my dad with his endless tea breaks and juggling – quite literally – of crockery. We stalked into the empty foyer. Mum smashed her hand down on the bell on the scarred wooden reception desk. Pablo, the owner, shuffled into view, a face like thunder.

'I tell you before.' Pablo pointed a gnarled finger at Mum, 'He working. You cannot visit during working hours. Had to chambermaid whole room again!'

A smirk played at Mum's lip. I wanted the ground to open and swallow me up: *Mum and Dad... Here? When he was on duty? Eeeurgh.*

'Oh, do grow up, Elizabeth,' Mum drawled, amused, taking in my horrified expression. 'Besides, you can talk!'

My mouth dropped wide open: was my mother actually making a joke about my situation? This was hardly the time! But before I could tell her off, Mum was arguing with Pablo, pushing past him towards the kitchen.

'Family emergency,' Mum said. Then when that didn't work: 'Get out of my way before I knock you down!'

Perplexed, Pablo finally got out of the way. Though not a particularly large or meaty man, Pablo was at least a foot taller than my mother. She couldn't have knocked him down with a hammer in hand.

'Thank you.' My mother said, before barking at me:

'Come on, Lizzie!'

We clattered down the steep steps to the subterranean, window-less kitchen where my father worked. A CD player was blaring some old band; he had terrible taste just like Mum. It was so loud Dad just about hit the ceiling when Mum tapped him on the shoulder. He was pleased to see us, though that was short-lived.

'How could you be so stupid, Lizzie?' Dad sighed.

'Don't talk to her like that!' Mum's eyes almost bulged out their sockets, she was that angry. 'Besides anything, you're a bloody hypocrite. We had Lizzie not much older than she is now!'

'That's different.' Dad said, 'We were always going to stay here.'

'Speak for yourself.' Mum scoffed, 'I had plans. I got side-tracked.'

'By me I suppose?' Dad countered. I'd heard them have this argument a million times before.

'Not really. You didn't stick around long enough, Dan!'

Dad's face twisted as if he'd swallowed several wasps. *Ouch.* I watched them argue, disbelieving. I'd never imagined this reaction from Mum. I'd expected her to be the disappointed one, the one who would bawl me out for it. I had misjudged her.

'Lizzie, you have plans...' Dad began, but one look from Mum silenced him.

'It has to be her decision, Dan.' Mum said. 'Whatever I think, you think, the other girls think ... It's irrelevant!'

'What about the baby's father?' Dad said.

Mum visibly deflated. It was obvious she'd forgotten about Mike. With a sudden pang, I realised I had too. I'd wanted to avoid thinking about his reaction; I was afraid what it might be. I couldn't believe he would be angry, but then I didn't believe he would welcome the news, either. I knew whatever I said or whatever his reply might be, I would be left with disappointment.

'You need to tell him.' Mum said to me.

I wanted to argue with her, but she would never allow me to simply keep my mouth shut. Mum had told us never to hide, to hold our heads up high. So what if the rest of the world saw the scally father, the chain-smoking mother, the endless brood of children? Every time she'd had to go seeking help at the likes of Social Services, someone would say, in accusing fashion, *why have so many children if you can't support them?* Except it's never as simple as that. Mum had never set out to drain the state. Life gets in the way and re-arranges things for us all. Besides, should our decisions be based on what others thought? Of course not. You just have to do what you can. Mum had raised us all to be honest and to do our best, too. What else was there?

'I'll tell him tomorrow.' I found myself saying.

'Just get it over with, sweetheart'. Mum saw me baulk at this and her expression softened. She gave me a quick hug for reassurance.

I felt stronger immediately. 'Okay, today.'

Lucy V Hay

Thirty-two

The day felt like a whirlwind. Barely an hour past after telling my dad, I was seated in Francis' living room with Mike. Over tea the colour of dishwater in the kitchen, Mum and Francis sat together in the kitchen. The radio was turned off on Mum's insistence, 'just in case'.

'Your father went mad when I told him I was expecting you,' Mum had said on the way to Mike's. 'Of course, he reckoned it was my fault; I had planned it; I was trying to 'trap' him… Though exactly how he could never answer. Anyone would have thought he had some big career planned.'

'You didn't live together then?' This was news to me.

'Oh, no. I was still with GanGan back then. Your Dad and I had had Amanda as well before we set up home together.' Mum said, negotiating the road. 'And then of course he was gone again more or less after Sal and Hannah, even before we had the twins. Not that he could stay away for long.'

'Why do you put up with him?' I asked, cringing at the thought of the answer. Whatever his faults, he was still my dad. But even so, I felt I needed to know.

'I love him, I suppose.' Mum said. There was absolutely no hint of the starry-eyed teen about her as she said it, either. 'There were times I tried to break it off, but my heart was never in it. Besides, perhaps I…'

'…Okay, okay.' I said hurriedly, sure Mum was going

to say something embarrassing about sex or similar. The thought of them together just made me heave. They'd never gone to any particular effort to hide their sex life. I'd come home to the squeaking of bedsprings even in the middle of the day countless times. It got to the point that if I had friends over, I'd leave them outside first and check. Why couldn't I just have normal parents, ones that actually lived together and couldn't stand each other? *Everyone else did!*

'I was going to say, perhaps I liked my independence.' Mum said. 'Raising you girls my way, no interference. A man who was interested in us all, supported us when he could, yet kept his distance. I was a single Mum, but not. Maybe I felt like I had the best of both worlds?'

I had always been so focused on Dad not being there twenty-four-seven. Now I thought of it, I could see how ridiculous my assumption was: my mother, a victim? Mad. But it had never occurred to me to the situation might suit her, or even suit them both.

'But I also had the worst of both worlds.' Mum continued as she drew the car up outside Mike's. She pulled the handbrake, turned off the ignition.

'But you just said…?' I trailed off, confused.

'Paradox.' Mum said.

That word again. I remembered the eleven-year-old Shona and her belief it was possible to have choices and yet still be destined to do certain things. Mrs. Jenkin-No-S would have sat both of us down that night at Shona's parents and presented us with a dictionary (while insisting on a nip of vodka herself). 'To know a word is to be able to define a word' as she was so fond of saying.

But I could already define the word 'paradox': 'A seemingly contradictory statement that is nonetheless true'. The word was derived from the Latin 'pardoxum' or Greek, 'paradoxon', meaning 'conflicting with expectation'. But even knowing the word didn't make it easier to understand when it was applied to real life and real situations.

'It will be okay, won't it Mum?' I said. All of a sudden, I needed her support and her approval, like a child.

Only I wasn't a child any longer … I was having one of my own.

Mum smiled. 'That, I can promise.'

But her words did not fill me with comfort, as I'd hoped they would. Really, I wanted her to make the decision for me. But she couldn't; only I could.

I broke the news to Mike. I explained it all: how both of us were to blame for not using contraception; how I'd not been able to face the doctor; how I'd not had the twenty pounds necessary to buy the morning after pill; how we'd never even talked about what had happened the night he got thrown out of the pub. I finished, hoping he wouldn't start with the accusations, or anger. I needn't have worried; Mike listened with wide eyes, all too aware of my mother and his father in the next room.

'What next, then?' Mike said.

'I'm not sure.' I said, 'I was hoping you would tell me how you felt?'

Mike shrugged. 'Well, obviously I'm not happy about it.'

I felt a twinge of hurt. In my imagination's version, the father of my child would be overjoyed and impressed somehow, as if I had done something clever. But really, I couldn't blame Mike; I had not exactly been thrilled about the pregnancy either. I supposed it was his choice of words: *Obviously I'm not happy about it*. As if the news was something really irritating, like visiting boring relatives or having to write an essay for college.

'Nor am I.'

I tried to keep a lid on the irritation bubbling in my stomach. It threatened to travel up my throat and burst out my mouth in the form of angry words. Losing my temper now would help no one.

'So, what are you going to do?'

Mike's enquiry was bald. So, it was up to me. Not what were 'we' going to do. Instead, it would be my decision – and mine alone. And not because he respected my right to choose either, but because he'd just rather not deal with it. *Typical Mike.*

In that moment, I felt something click in my head. What was my gut instinct? Now had to be one of those times I relied on it. I remembered my mother's words in the car park, *'You know what options are available. What you mean is, you can't decide.'*

'I'm keeping it.' I said.

The words sounded almost unreal to my own ears, yet as soon as I uttered them aloud, I knew it was the right decision somehow. This was my choice. This was what I wanted and needed. I could figure out university and all the other life stuff later. It wasn't going anywhere.

Mike's face remained impassive, like he was made of stone. His cold stare, never wavered. Guilt immediately pierced my heart. What if he didn't want the child? Did I have the right to have the baby, regardless of what he felt? But I was the one who would have to deal with the consequences, no matter what Mike chose to do next. He didn't have to stay. He could opt out, walk away whenever he wanted. I was the one who was truly affected by all this.

'Are you okay with that?' I dared to ask, virtually holding my breath.

'I guess I'll have to be.' He sighed.

What an anti-climax. About twenty minutes later, Mum came and fetched me from the front room, we went home. Getting in the car, I looked back at Mike's house and saw the window was empty. He hadn't waited there, to wave.

Thirty-three

As planned, Mike went to university a few weeks after my announcement. 'It's better this way' my parents and Francis said, which I echoed, knowing they were right, yet not feeling it at all.

I stayed at home, taking a job with Mr. Edwards at the local chemists and hiding my growing bump beneath long cardigans and under the counter from my employer. At least I could always pick up my Mum's prescriptions for her.

Mike was in contact most days. Snapchat messages mostly, decorated with hearts. The odd phone call. Every time he'd say a hurried 'I love you' and ring off. I wasn't sure if I believed him, or whether he believed the words himself. Was it something he just said, because he felt he had to? And was the same true for me?

Shona too trotted off to university. Just a few weeks in, I realised she'd dropped me like a stone. Promised phone calls never happened; visits never came. Our friendships were acted out on Twitter and WhatsApp instead. She told me how much she missed me and how I should come and see her … But with so little money and a baby to save for, this was impossible for me. As my stomach grew, her invites came less and less.

It was hard to find new friends: it was as if all the teenagers around our way had vanished. Perhaps most had? Going to university was the perfect escape route. I knew no other girl even close to my age having a baby. I went to a couple of antenatal classes in town but discovered the only Mums-To-Be there were old – thirties and forties even – and more than a bit weird. The nurse or midwife (or whatever she was) patronised us, asking to us to hold plastic dolls during 'circle time'. One got us to tell everyone our hopes for when the baby came and how we feel our lives might change. I tried not to laugh as I heard them all go on about how wonderful their lives were going to be. Had they never heard of varicose veins or postnatal depression? Had they ever considered their children might be twenty-four carat brats or their husbands might leave them?

By the time the midwife-whatever got to me, it was the end of the session and I felt relief. I had absolutely no idea how my life would change for the better. I would have a baby, sure. That bit I was almost looking forward to. But the lack of money terrified me and babies were expensive. And what was my future, now? I had no idea how my life would work with a child in tow; it was as if my whole life had a massive question mark hanging over it.

At home, tensions were high. Amanda had screwed up her qualification in health and beauty. It turned out she'd barely turned up for class at all and had been hiding letters from Mum, down the side of her bed. Mum had gone nuclear and grounded Amanda for about seventeen years. Not that this bothered my sister, of course. Amanda still managed to go to Open Mic night at the pub in town every Tuesday. First, she would wait for Mum to go to bed, then she'd climb out the window, using the dead apple tree near the house to make her escape. Then Amanda would walk the miles necessary; there and back. I'd hear her clamber into bed at three in the morning, smelling of gin and giggling.

Sal had received glittering results for her exams – as predicted – and was now at the local college doing maths and all the sciences. As far as she was concerned, it was now official she was better than the rest of us, but especially me. Hannah began her own exams and kept changing her options every five minutes, driving Mum mad with numerous calls to the school principal. As for the twins… They were just the twins. They discovered a mewling bag in a brook near the house. Inside, were seven very damp kittens. Mum told the twins they couldn't keep them. She promised to put a card up in the local post office, but the card never materialised. Before long all seven of the kittens were full-on cats and sleeping under mum's bed with her own favourite feline, Monty.

My pregnancy progressed as it should. Being young and having a mother as experienced as mine, it couldn't really have gone any other way, without extreme bad luck. Never a big eater before, I discovered I was ravenous most of the time, with salt and vinegar crisps, orange juice, chocolate and even chunks of ice carved out of the freezer on my constant hit list.

Before long, I looked as if I had swallowed a beach ball. I put weight on rapidly on my stomach and legs; my small frame felt suddenly huge. To my dismay, my belly soon looked like a road map of red lines. I had them under my arms and on my thighs too. I became convinced I was massive, which was not helped by Mike when he came to visit at weekends and during university holidays.

'You can hardly even tell you're pregnant from this angle.' He said as I stood nearby, my back to him.

'Thanks a lot!' I said, spikes of sarcasm flying through the air.

'It was supposed to be a compliment!'

That was the way it was between us. There was always a disagreement bubbling under, just ready to erupt. A cruel streak had surfaced in Mike I hadn't noticed before: there were lots of subtle put-downs and the occasional outright jibe. When we were alone, he'd pinch me or twist my arm, then insist he had never done so. Sometimes – and usually when the rest of the family were out - he even pinned me down and yelled in my face, insisting I wasn't listening to him. Everything I said or did he called into question, making me doubt myself.

When I asked him why he was doing it, he denied all knowledge. Angry and confused, I caused arguments of my own. This only played directly to his belief everything was my fault. In contrast, Mike cosied up to my sisters, flattering them with pleasantries and compliments, the exact opposite of what he was giving me. Whenever he and I argued, he'd appeal to Hannah in particular, who - still just a little girl in so many ways and so eager to please - would always side with him: *yes, it was me, not him.* The others would do the same. I felt alone again.

At least I didn't have to see so much of Francis. Mike was with us most of the time he wasn't at university. Before the baby arrived, we barely saw the old man as he was confined to the end of the phone instead. I soon wished Mike were the same. It was so weird: I'd spend weeks just waiting to see him; yet when he was with me, I'd wish he would leave again. Sometimes, usually very early in the morning as I listened to Mike snore softly next me, I wondered if we were just acting out parts. I didn't want to stop Mike from knowing his own kid; he didn't want to be the one who left his pregnant girlfriend.

Yet at the same time, I couldn't imagine a future without Mike in it, either. I wanted the little house; I wanted more children; I wanted my own career. Could I have any of those things without him? Who else would have me? Maybe I should put up and shut up, make do with what I had.

Nothing seemed certain. I just wanted someone, anyone, to help me formulate a plan … Or better still, figure it all out for me, let me know what I would be doing a year from now! Perhaps I would feel better once the baby arrived?

As I turned out, I didn't have as long to wait as I thought.

Thirty-four

The baby was a month early.

There was chaos and panic as my waters broke at home. A weekend, Mike was there. Mum tried to calm me, telling me thirty-six weeks' gestation was fine for some babies. But I refused to calm down. I shrieked at her, demanding to know how she would know? Her babies were always late!

Dad looked after the girls and Mum drove me and Mike to the hospital. Mike was both scared and sulking, for I'd told him some weeks before that I wanted Mum present at the birth as well. He had attempted to persuade me otherwise many times already, telling me he 'should be enough for me'. But what if he fainted or ran out, unable to handle it? What if he said stupid things or stressed me out? I knew I needed someone present I could count on – like Mum - no matter how many tantrums Mike pulled about it.

At the hospital, a midwife reassured me my mother was right; thirty-seven weeks was considered 'on time' so in reality, my baby was only a week early. I felt my stress levels decrease. The pain of labour went down a little as I stopped panicking, though it was still a more excruciating experience than I had ever contemplated. Mum coaxed me to breathe through it, showing me how and holding my hand. Mike stood by on the sidelines, hands deep in his pockets. I had wondered if I would feel sorry for him beforehand, but I was too busy I had no time to worry about that. Even Mum seemed far away somehow, even though I had had no drugs. It was just me and the baby.

I had not asked if I was carrying a boy or a girl; I'd wanted the surprise. Mike had felt sure the child would be a boy and had even picked out a name: Tommy. Not wanting more arguments, I'd decided I would see the child for who he or she was and name it on the day. Now I couldn't wait to see the little one's face and it kept me going through the pain. I realised: despite all the uncertainty and my worries for the future, I wanted this child and I couldn't wait to be a mother.

The labour was long and hard work. Two shifts of midwives shuffled in and out, checking me and monitoring the baby, talking to Mum as if I was an idiot. I knew labour could be long, but after more than fourteen hours with contractions every three minutes, I began to feel desperate at the slow progress. Would it ever finish?

Then something changed. There were shouts and the crash of bed railings. Mum was trying to tell me something: *baby in distress.* Panic pierced my heart all over again: could my baby die? Mike was suddenly beside me, holding my hand. Then he disappeared again. The midwife was talking at me, saying they needed to get me prepped for theatre and I mustn't worry … This happens all the time; the baby's tired; they just need to give him or her a helping hand.

But all her words ran together and all I could really hear was the spinning of bed wheels; the mutterings of a consultant and the midwives; my Mum's hurried reassurances and someone sobbing, which I realised later was me.

Daisy Heather Carmichael was born at one twelve am, weighing just under five and a half pounds and screaming her heart out.

'Nothing wrong with those lungs!' the consultant joked, sewing me up.

Still lying down and staring up at the hospital's white tiled ceiling, relief flooded through me to hear her cries.

Mum started crying too.

'Oh Lizzie, she looks just like you!'

Seconds later a theatre nurse with a big smile on her face presented Daisy to me in a pink blanket: 'You have a daughter.'

A daughter. What fantastic words. Holding her for the first time, I took in her delicate features, which were twisted up as if she were in the biggest of huffs. I couldn't help but laugh, then regretted it. My insides felt red raw.

As they wheeled us back to the ward, I caught sight of Mike slumped in a plastic chair near maternity. I felt sorry he hadn't been there to see her born, too. But as the panicked rush for theatre had started, he'd been left behind somewhere.

'I'll leave you two alone for a bit.' Mum said brightly.

Mike peered at the tiny pink bundle. 'She's okay?'

I nodded. 'I thought … Daisy?'

Mike's upper lip immediately curled. 'How about Olivia?'

'Please, Mike.' I said, desperately tired.

'Fine.' He replied. 'As usual I don't count for anything.'

'No, that's not true.' I said, tears pricking my eyelids. This was a special moment. How could he want an argument now?

But Mike could barely look at me. He went back to staring out of the maternity ward window, down on to the concrete car park below. I was confused by his reaction. Why couldn't I name the baby? He'd never wanted a particular girl's name. As ever, he just wanted it his way.

I had to stay in hospital for the next four days. Mum had to go home to look after the rest of the girls, but Mike popped in a couple of time. He never brought a gift for Daisy, like the other new dads on the ward. An empty vase stood on my nightstand and there were no toys placed in Daisy's crib.

Francis came and tried to extend nicotine-stained fingers near her mouth. I managed to stop him when I said I needed to feed her. Embarrassed, Francis withdrew and said he would come back another time but never did. I finally got to meet Mike's mother Maria, who arrived with helium balloons and an almost hysterical smile on her face, dragging Mike's half-brother James behind her.

'You're an uncle now!' She kept exclaiming. James seemed disinterested and just like his older brother, spent most of his time staring down at the car park.

Perhaps most surprising of all, Shona turned up. She'd been down for the weekend at her parents', though she hadn't told me. She came in with a large pink teddy for the baby that was far too fluffy for a newborn.

'So, how you been, anyway?' She said, her expression guarded.

I would have laughed at the stupid question, but I knew it would hurt too much. I wanted to tell her my entire life and outlook had changed; I wanted to say that she might have been the one who had 'got out', but I was the one who had outgrown her. But instead I said:

'Fine, thanks.'

Mum arrived on the last day just as I was signing my discharge papers. Mum regaled me with how she'd moved the girls around, so I could have the room I'd previously shared with Amanda to myself, with Daisy. Apparently, Hannah was happy enough to share with the twins now and they'd been bribed with a new set of pink bunkbeds. Amanda had never cared where she slept; it was only Sal whose nose was out of joint, complaining that Amanda spent too much time spraying perfume when she was trying to study. I listened to Mum as I shuffled out to the car like a little old lady, holding the baby. I wondered why Mike had not come to get us as well.

'I did ask him.' Mum said.

'What did he say?' I enquired, almost dreading the answer.

'Francis said he couldn't come to the phone, he was sleeping off a bender.' Mum said grimly. 'Wetting the baby's head maybe.'

A chink of hope opened in my heart: perhaps if Mike was celebrating Daisy's birth, he was finally getting used to the idea of being a dad? But a cynical voice in the back of my head crushed it: *or he's just doing what he's always done.*

I'd never known where I stood with Mike. He'd always blocked my attempts to find out, making me guess instead. When I inevitably got things wrong because I was not a mind reader, it was all my fault.

I wondered if I could stand a lifetime of it. Looking at Daisy's face, I figured I would have to. Mike was her father and nothing could change that fact now. I just had to make the best of it.

For her sake.

Thirty-five

Mike finally turned up three days after I came home from the hospital, six days after Daisy's birth. His 'weekend away' had become a week, all with the university's permission.

'It's not every day you become a dad.' Mike joked.

So why not see your baby every day, then? I wanted to say but didn't. This had become the story of my life: I would want to ask Mike something, but feared an argument, so would keep my mouth shut… Yet somehow, I still ended up in arguments with him anyway. It was so weird. I didn't believe I was a particularly argumentative or difficult person, but Mike seemed to think I was … So, did that make it true? I couldn't decide.

Mike went back to university. I settled into the routine motherhood brings with it. Feeding, changing, washing and in my case, healing. I looked in the mirror and saw the saggy skin of my belly, the black stitches that now held it together. My breasts, filled with milk, were sore and massive. My complexion was ghost-white, my hair greasy. I felt a million years old and looked it. I didn't recognise my own body. Mum told me everything would change back, but I wasn't convinced. I never remembered Mum having so much as a stretchmark; even as big as she got with the twins, yet I was covered with them. I felt like I was spoiled, somehow.

In comparison, Daisy was the perfect baby. She was bright, cheerful, always smiling. I found breastfeeding easy as she took to it so well. She slept lots, when I let her. I was so paranoid she might die from cot death if she slept too long, I kept waking her up. Mum told me I had to relax, that Daisy would let me know if there was a problem, but I just kept worrying. I was young! If I got things wrong, there must be people willing to take her away like a shot? Mum told me again and again this wasn't true. I had a good support network and Social Services never took children away on a whim. Yet everywhere I saw the bogeyman of the authorities, just waiting for me to slip up and snatch my child from my arms.

Money was tight. It wasn't long before I had to give up my part-time job at the chemist's and sign on, instead. I didn't want to, but I simply could not do enough hours to justify the childcare. Mum had her own work and childcare difficulties. She did manage to pick up a permanent job at a bar near the seafront, but it meant her working nights. I became the official babysitter of the twins, so at least one of us could stay in work. Amanda and Hannah took me seriously, even if Sal was as salty as ever.

Mike would ring and tell me about things that had happened at university. He'd never ask what I had been up to, only tacking on that all-important question when he remembered:

'How's the baby?' He'd say. Never Daisy. Always 'the baby'.

'Fine.' I'd say.

'Good.'

If I'd thought fatherhood might change Mike, I was disappointed. He'd hold her, or play with her for a few moments, but he'd get bored. He didn't want to help feed her, bathe her, or take her for a walk. If he noticed her nappy was dirty, he would hand her straight back to me. He gave me no money for her either. Instead, he'd spend his cash on going to the pub, or gigs, or on gadgets like a new phone. If

I complained, he'd say, 'But I'm a student!' He'd then persuade me that it was better he didn't get into more debt on his loan, so when he left we'd have more money. (Like an idiot, I heard 'when' and figured this meant he would take responsibility 'later', after uni, so let him get away with it).

One thing Mike did love was showing Daisy off to his friends. He'd turn up at Francis' with someone and phone me, to come over. I always dropped everything and rushed over there with her. He was quite the celebrity with his uni mates: a dad! At his age! And Daisy was so cute! I felt a pang of envy that none of my old college friends wanted to see her or me in the same way. Even so, after an hour – never much longer – Daisy was handed back to me. In body language, rather than words, they'd let me know we would no longer be required. Like typical students, they were off to the pub, but I was never invited.

More time passed. My body did change back to normal as Mum had promised, so I became a little more confident, as well as bored. I started to wonder what would happen next. Why shouldn't I? Daisy was almost one and already tottering about mum's kitchen like a pro. I had been patient. I had been understanding. Mike had not had to give up anything … He hadn't had to *do* anything! It had all fallen to me. The time felt right to ask where I stood and when we could be a proper family at last.

'I thought we could get our own place, with Daisy?' We were lying in my cramped single bed, Daisy in her cot. I'd waited for him to come back for the weekend, rather than ask him over the phone.

Even in the moonlight through the crack in the curtains, the panic in Mike's eyes was unmistakable. 'But I've got university.'

'I know.'

I suppressed a sigh. I had known this would not be easy. I just had to stick to the lines I had rehearsed in my head a thousand times that week.

'We would come with you, live near the university. I could get a job, Daisy could go to nursery?'

'It'll be my third year, I'll have my finals.'

'I don't understand.'

He tutted, as if I was stupid. 'Well, I can hardly study in peace with a crying baby in the house, can I? What if I fail? Then all this would be for nothing.'

Hot anger coursed through me. *All this??* What was that supposed to mean! I had been the one who had made all the sacrifices, not him! Daisy was not just a 'crying baby', she was his daughter. Sure she cried, but no more than average. She was a sweet-natured girl, with only the occasional flares of temper, which Mike would know if he spent more time with her. But I swallowed my fury down – as usual – even though I wanted to strangle the life out of him.

'We could manage.' I clenched my teeth.

'Tamsin said most relationships fail because of pressurised circumstances.' Mike said, his manner airy. 'Money, timing, that sort of thing.'

Tamsin again. She was a friend of Mike's from university; they shared a module in psychology together. She had come down with him a couple of times and stayed at Francis'. Like all his other mates, she'd gone on about Daisy: what a gorgeous little thing she was, how clever she was. That had been pretty standard, but I'd found it weird how Tamsin had showered me with compliments too. What was all that about? Tamsin was a plain, freckled girl with a nice smile and round face. She reminded me of Chloe Bensham from Year 9, a fat girl who had always complimented others in the unsuccessful hope she would receive some praise back.

I'd thanked Tamsin but noted there had been a strange glint in her eye. I couldn't place it at the time. Alone at home with Daisy later, I had wondered if it had been guilt? But for all his faults, Mike was not a cheat. *Was he?* Even if he was, I was better-looking than Tamsin. He wouldn't go off with her, surely. Like Shona always said, 'Why have beef burger when you got prime steak at home?' But he kept saying her name, over and over. Mike only talked about people he really liked. I knew, deep down, he must have a thing for her.

'... This has got nothing to do with Tamsin.' My face was in darkness, so he couldn't see my sour expression.

I heard Mike blow out his cheeks. 'Don't start that again.'

'Start what?' I countered, 'For God's sake Mike, I'm talking about our future here... Ours and Daisy's! I've been waiting here, in limbo, for you. I just want to know what happens next! That is not unreasonable.'

There: I said it.

Mike attempted to roll over, turn his back on me. 'I can't talk to you when you're being like this.'

'Being like what?'

I wasn't about to let this go. I'd had enough of being left dangling.

'You're being childish.' Mike said.

'Me, childish??' My volume rose. I forgot about the rest of the house, asleep. A light on the landing came on, but I barely noticed. '*You're* the one who won't face up to his responsibilities!'

'Shut up!' Sal yelled across the landing from her bedroom.

We paused, waiting for the light to go off again. It did, so we resumed where we'd let off, though quieter.

'I'm a student.' Mike reminded me for the hundredth time.

'There are men and women up and down the country who are parents and students,' I hissed, 'What do you think they do, put their kids in storage? They seem to manage ... Maybe because they don't have someone as stupid as me, hanging around and waiting for you to get off your arse!'

Suddenly Mike sat up. He grabbed my arm and twisted it, pulling me towards him in the bed. I knew his face was close against mine; I could feel his breath on my face. My heartbeat quickened a step, frightened. He said nothing; he knew he was intimidating me.

'Mike, don't.' I hated how small my voice sounded in the dark.

He let go and propelled me away from him. My back hit the plaster of the wall behind me. He yanked the duvet away, pulling it around himself. I was left in the cold and damp.

'I'm going to sleep.' He declared.

That was it for him, case closed. I sat up on the bed, smarting every bit as much as the bruise that was raising on my arm.

Enough was enough.

Thirty-six

The morning came. Neither the previous night nor the idea of us all living together was mentioned again. Mum clocked the hostility between Mike and I at the breakfast table, but I dodged even her most probing questions. I knew what she thought, anyway. She reckoned I was better off without Mike. Maybe she was right. My dad had never been Father of the Year, but he'd always been there: birthdays, Christmases, school plays and sports days. He'd was interested in us, loved us. Mike only wanted me and Daisy when it suited him, when he wasn't paying.

There was a part of me that wanted him out, gone. But the other half of me was afraid. I looked across at my daughter, sleeping in her crib. Did I have the right to send her dad away, just because I didn't like or want him anymore? What if she blamed me for all this? I couldn't decide anymore if was being responsible, or a doormat. I was also scared of facing life alone as a single parent. Okay, technically I was one already, but at least Mike had (kind of) stood by me. Who else would have me? I had made my bed and now I had to lie on it, as the saying went. With Mike, it seemed. I didn't have any other choice.

I had to do something.

I'd read enough women's magazines and seen enough daytime television chat shows. The advice ladled out by them was simple: work out what you want and tell him.

Don't make him guess, because he won't. I remembered Nora, my mum's teaching friend coming to the house; it was during yet another bad patch between Mum and Dad when I was younger. They'd discussed Mum and Dad's relationship in hushed tones as I'd eavesdropped.

'Things are so bad… He has no idea how bad they are.' Mum said.

Nora had sucked her breath in her over her teeth. I'd known this was significant somehow, but not why. But I knew now: Mum had tried to tell Dad what the problem was, but he just wasn't listening … like Mike wasn't listening to me now. I'd told him waiting for him was no longer working for me; that I wanted us to live together; that I wanted us to be a proper family at last. I had been ignored.

Now it was time for phase two.

I'd grown up in a house of ultimatums, thanks to my mother: clean your bedroom or you're grounded. Eat your breakfast or you're grounded. Stop arguing with your sisters or you're grounded. Unlike many parents', these were not idle threats either. My mother always followed through and groundings could be the worst ever. She didn't just send us to our rooms, she put us to work. The dreaded bathroom was one of the worst, especially after Amanda and all her potions had been in there. Also, humungous piles of ironing and even gardening if it was sunny. Us kids did all we could to avoid a grounding, even the twins. Aged four, they'd had to scrub the front doorstep with two small toothbrushes. (Mum hadn't been able to think of how else to punish them for ripping up the corner of the carpet in the hall just to see what was underneath).

So as far as I was concerned, ultimatums were part of relationships. I decided I would tell Mike he needed to take responsibility for me and Daisy, or it was over between us. On the surface, it seemed like a good plan. After all, why would he step up and do what was he supposed to, if I took care of everything? It seemed foolproof. Even if he forced me to carry out my threat, he would soon miss me and Daisy. All I would have to do is bide my time and wait for him to come crawling back.

Wouldn't he?

Thirty-seven

Another university holiday rolled around. Me and Daisy went to Francis' with Mike, for once. I told him I wanted her to spend some time with her grandfather. In reality, the thought of Francis breathing his gross odours near my daughter made me cringe a little. He didn't appear to have a clue what to do with Daisy either. I wondered how Mike had survived past babyhood. Francis kept shaking his car keys at her, like she was a dog or something. He'd apparently not noticed Daisy was now nearly one, walking and had a vocabulary of about ten or fifteen words. These included 'Mummy', 'Drink?' and 'Yeah man!' (Amanda had taught her it. Daisy thought was one word). Good-tempered as always, Daisy would look at Francis wide-eyed before racing off to the television and flicking through channels, leaving smeared handprints across the screen, pointing to things she liked.

I was itching to deliver Mike my ultimatum but knew I couldn't do it as soon as I got there. I had to wait for the most opportune moment, just like the magazines and chat shows suggested. By the third day, one had still not arrived. Mike was typically distant, always snapchatting or playing video games. I had grown bored and Daisy kept asking when we were going home. She missed the hustle and bustle of the house, the endless blaring noise of my sisters and even my mum's shouting. We especially missed her cooking: Francis and Mike barely ate enough to keep a mouse alive between them. I found myself sneaking Daisy off to the bakery to buy cheese and onion pasties; hardly healthy and I was running short of money. So, on the fourth day, I called my mum and told her we were coming home that afternoon. I'd given myself a deadline.

It was now or never.

I suggested to Mike we take Daisy to the swings. Walking past the old broken-down bandstand together, I noted the autumn leaves on the ground and the chill in the air. Mike would be going back to university for his final year soon. He was planning on living with his friends, like so many students. I hadn't been bothered until I discovered one of these friends was Tamsin. I had pretended this was no problem, though panic had lanced through me. I knew I had to find a way of ensuring Tamsin and Mike did not share the same house.

This would be it.

'I need more.' I had not thought I would be delivering my ultimatum in a child's play park as my daughter went up and down a graffittied slide.

Mike turned to me, a question mark on his face. I took a deep breath.

'If you can't give it to us, then we're over.' I felt the pent-up frustration of the past couple of years burst inside me.

Mike stared at his shoes, hands in his pockets. I willed him to plead with me, tell me it could all be different. I wanted him to realise what he'd (not) done for his family… But that he could fix it. I wanted him to suggest we go back to Francis' and work out how to make it all work. Top of my list would be his ditching the shared house (or more crucially, Tamsin) and finding a flat together where he went to university. In planning for this moment, I had already asked for nursery brochures and checked out the local area around Mike's uni on various maps and street views. I'd already moved there and set up home with him and Daisy, in my head.

But none of this was said.

'Maybe it is the end of the line for us.' Mike said.

I sighed. So, he would have to find out the hard way, then. 'Okay.'

We walked back to Francis' house, Daisy swinging between us from our hands. *He will miss this*, I thought. *He will realise his mistake, come back to us, be the partner and father we both deserve.*

I should have known it wouldn't work out like that.

Thirty-eight

I found myself waiting again. Days later, Mike was back at university and in his house share. Though I was wild with jealousy inside at the thought of him living with Tamsin, I told myself it was just a minor setback. Mike would soon realise what he was missing out on, if not with me, then his own daughter. *Right??*

Though we were no longer officially together, Mike still rang. He still wanted to see Daisy when he came back for weekends. I would go and see him at Francis' and occasionally stay over. I always had the spare room, with Daisy in the fold-up travel cot. Even so, Mike would sneak in to my bed during the night and I would let him. I felt sure things were going the way they were 'supposed' to … It was just taking longer than I expected.

Two or three months into this relationship (that was apparently not a relationship), Mike dropped his bombshell. He and I were in bed together at Francis'. I heard the tone of his mobile, but before I could grab it to give it to him, he snatched it up off the bedside table. He got out of bed, still naked. He went through to the bathroom, talking in a low voice. I knew immediately something was up.

'Who was that?' I demanded. Somehow, I knew who it was.

He refused to answer at first. He pulled on his clothes, turning his back.

I wanted to be wrong. 'You're seeing Tamsin, aren't you?'

'What do you want me to say?' Mike's voice was flat, which somehow made it worse.

It was as bad as I'd feared. They'd got together the first night they'd moved into the house share. He came out with the usual crap: he hadn't meant for it to happen, blah blah blah. Even worse, he told me Tamsin was his best friend. He said that things were just so easy with her, in a way they never had been with me. Each word was like he stabbed me in the heart. I couldn't believe it. I had delivered Mike, gift-wrapped to this girl! I asked him why he'd cheated on Tamsin, then? He'd shrugged. He said he wanted to see Daisy, he was worried I might not let him. Besides, who would turn sex down when it was handed on a plate?

I returned home with Daisy, resolving never to speak to Mike again. I was disgusted, both with him and myself. I realised my mistake, too: if I'd wanted Mike back, I should have made him work his way back to us. I'd basically let him go and then come back on a whim, just as I always had! Worse, in fact, because now he had two girlfriends on the go!

Mum and Dad could see I was upset, but everyone trod eggshells around me, sure I would open up when I was ready. But I didn't trust myself to speak, for fear of it all coming flooding out. I knew I deserved better, but then so did Tamsin. I became obsessed with the thought of her. I called up her Instagram profile and stared at pictures of her. Mike was in some of them. *How could this have happened?*

At first, I felt sure I should tell her, 'save' her from Mike – once a cheat, always a cheat. Then resentment eclipsed my good sense. Tamsin knew Mike and I had a baby together. As his supposed 'best friend', she presumably knew we'd had problems with our relationship. Yet here she was, first chance she got, getting in the way of us making it work!

What kind of girl was she? *Clearly not a nice one.*

So, I formed a new plan. I would play the Mistress, if that's what it took. Tamsin had to get boring for him, eventually. Mike only had six or seven months of university left. He and Tamsin were bound to go their separate ways afterwards? I had the trump card: Daisy. Mike was Daisy's father. I could wait this out. I felt I had to: I had invested too much in this situation. I had invested too much for it all to fall apart at the final hurdle. I had to do the right thing by my daughter and wait just that little bit longer, suffer this humiliation.

For Daisy.

Thirty-nine

'I've got something to tell you, Lizzie.'

Mum and Dad hadn't realised Mike and I had technically split up, since I had still said nothing. They'd thought the break in Mike's visits when he went back for the third year at uni were just teething troubles. Then Mum saw Tamsin and Mike kissing in town during the Easter holidays. She sat in front of me at the kitchen table, sombre-faced. She said she'd agonised over whether she should tell me.

I sighed. 'It's not like that.'

I felt even worse, having to tell Mum it actually me who was the 'other woman', not Tamsin. Mum said very little, but I could tell from her pinched-faced expression she didn't approve.

'That boy always gets his own way.' I could tell she wanted to say more. She drummed her fingers on the table, a classic sign she was trying to keep hold of herself. 'It's time you stood up for yourself. Show Daisy what real women are made of.'

I felt my own temper rise. 'Oh, you mean like you do, with me over Dad?'

Mum blew out her cheeks. She looked like she was counting to ten. 'Look, you're a grown up, a mother yourself now. You have to decide if this is really what you want, whether you're happy to be someone's dirty little secret … and whether you're happy Daisy will be, too.'

Then she left me to it, to puzzle it out myself.

Knowing Tamsin and Mike were together while he was away at university was harsh. It felt good to get one over on Tamsin, at first. It felt like she'd always been there, getting in-between me and Mike, taking Daisy's father away. But it was not long before shame replaced these thoughts. Tamsin seemed a nice girl; nicer than me and definitely nicer than Mike. She didn't deserve this and nor did I. Both of us could do better.

To take my mind off things, I started applying for universities. I looked around several and picked one about a hundred miles from home. It had an on-campus nursery for Daisy and good train links back to Exmorton. To my surprise, just a few weeks into the application process, I discovered I had an unconditional place. I could begin my course that September.

'What about Daisy?' Mum said.

I was adamant. 'I'm taking her with me.'

'It'll be hard.' Mum warned.

I nodded. 'I know.'

Mum's face cracked a wide smile. 'Good for you.'

Mike was less enthusiastic. He had decided he wanted to do a postgraduate course. When I suggested he come to the university I had chosen with me and Daisy, he told me he 'couldn't'. Apparently, they didn't do the postgraduate course he wanted. Another argument ensued, which ended abruptly when Tamsin called him on his mobile. Before he answered, I told him I'd bring Daisy to Francis' on Saturday so he could see her before he went back. But Mike waved me away like a parent would a small child. He shut the door to his dad's house as he answered the phone, pretending to Tamsin I was a charity collector. *More lies.*

Travelling back to my parents' on the bus with Daisy, I thought over what had just happened. It had taken that long, but it was like a lightbulb went on in my head. Mike was never going to be what I wanted him to be: a partner or father. He'd been allowed to do whatever he wanted. He'd not had to give up anything, or make any sacrifices. for the privilege. Of course, I had known this all along. But now I saw I had given him no incentive. The very fact he had needed one said it all, anyway.

Let Tamsin have him.

As promised, I took Daisy to Francis' the following Saturday. Walking through the streets from the bus station, I could feel my willpower slipping. I knew Tamsin was not at the house. But I had to do this.

Instead of letting myself in as I usually did, I rang the doorbell and waited outside with Daisy. A few moments passed before it opened. Mike stood there, looking puzzled. *Strike one.*

'Hi,' He'd done his hair, he was wearing aftershave. Perhaps he'd even been looking forward to seeing me?

I pushed another wave of guilt aside. 'Hi.'

Mike leant down next to Daisy. 'Hey, you, come to play at Daddy's?'

Daisy grinned and nodded, thumb in her mouth.

'All her stuff is in here – nappies, her cup, spare clothes.' I was business-like, handing over a pink rucksack.

Mike took it, his face a picture of utter bewilderment. *Strike two.*

'Are you not coming in?'

'No, I don't think so.' I said.

'Shopping, or something…?' Mike said hopefully, 'You look nice. Maybe we can talk later?'

We both knew what he meant: no talking would be involved, only sex. And afterwards everything would drag on, the way it always had. Now was the time to make the break.

I took a deep breath. 'No, I don't think so.'

Strike three.

Mike looked as if I'd hit him in the face, but as ever, said little else. I gave Daisy a quick kiss, told Mike I'd be back for her in a few hours and was on my way again, down the street.

I could feel Mike's puzzled stare boring into the back of my head, but I did not turn around. My heart thumped in my chest: *had I done the right thing?* I felt sure I had, but I was sad too. Why couldn't Mike have done what he was supposed to and either walked away, or stepped up? Why had he left me dangling so long? Why had I let him? There was something else there too now: relief.

I felt *free*.

As I turned the corner, my phone rang in my pocket. Wondering if it might be Mike, I took it out. But it wasn't his name on the screen...

ME

'Go after what it is that creates meaning in your life and then trust yourself to handle the stress that follows.'
Kelly McGonigal

Forty

A burst of white noise brought me to my senses. Pain lanced through my head and body at the sudden onslaught. Then another noise, this time a shrill ringing.

I lurched to one side, grabbing hold of the old paper towel dispenser to steady myself. Heat burst through my chest. I realised I was holding my breath. I tried to gulp in the stale air, but my chest felt restricted as if some great weight was sitting on it. *What was wrong with me?*

In my hand, the positive pregnancy test. I felt panic and despair hit me, but I wasn't allowed the distraction of either. The ringing continued. *The phone!*

I grabbed for my bag, spilling its contents across the grimy tiles. A book of poems; a pencil tin; a half-eaten chocolate bar; some random leaflets, a box of tampons – *you won't be needing them any time soon*, a cruel voice in the back of my mind heckled. Finally, there was my phone. A ridiculous amount of notifications and icons flashed on the screen, along with the name SAL. *What did she want?* She only ever contacted me when she wanted something. I couldn't talk to her.

Not today.

I pressed the red button and cancelled the call. Just as I'd done so, there was another call. This time the screen read MUM. What did I do now? Part of me wanted to answer the phone and spill my guts, but another part of me warned me not to. Why? I wasn't sure. What was it Mum always said, anyway? *Trust your gut instinct*. It was kind of ironic I was following her advice in not talking to her, but I couldn't worry about that now. I had other things to deal with. I pressed the red button again.

Immediately, the phone started ringing in my hand. I regarded it, incredulous. Two phone calls, one immediately after the other was strange, but not unheard of; Mum and Sal might even in the same room, both trying to track me down for some reason. It was an old strategy of Mum's when one of us went walkabout … So perhaps Amanda was being instructed to call me, too?

It wasn't Amanda. The phone screen read MIKE. There was no way he was with my mum and sisters! I could count the number of times they had all met on one hand. I never liked to take him back to the house. Sal was always making snide remarks and Hannah hung around him like a puppy dog. Besides, I shared a room with Amanda. I'd always thought it better we go back to his.

My thumb hovered over the buttons: 'accept' or 'reject'? I knew that pressing the green button would mean certain things would be set in motion. I had accepted the situation was happening. I accepted I had to tell someone. I even accepted there were other people who needed to be involved. But did that very first person have to be Mike? What would his reaction would be to the words, 'I'm pregnant'?

I pressed the red button.

The phone started ringing again. Agog, I regarded the LCD: now Shona's name flashed up. What were the odds of my mum, sister, Mike and Shona all calling me around the same time on any normal day, never mind the day I'd just taken a pregnancy test and found it to be positive? My mind whirled. Perhaps this was a sign I was meant to answer? But I'd never really believed in signs, fates or omens. As far as I was concerned, things happened or they didn't. How useful could Shona be, anyway? Like me, she had had unprotected sex before, but *unlike* me she had got away with it. Irritation and jealousy coursed through me at the thought of her (imagined) reaction. I pressed the red button, cutting her off.

But then it rang again: Sal was back. I cancelled her immediately this time. More ringing: Mum. I cut her off again. Mike's name flashed up; I cut him off again. Then Shona again! This was ridiculous. The phone kept ringing; I kept cutting them off. Again and again…

SAL…
MUM…
MIKE…
SHONA…

With a shriek of rage and without thinking, I hurled the phone away from me, across the room.

The handset hit the dirty tiled wall. It broke into two pieces, then fell into the water on the floor near the sinks and hand-dryer. Filled with instant regret, I rescued the phone from the stagnant puddle. The screen was waterlogged, the lights on the keypad were off. *Great.* I attempted to dry it on my clothes, then under the noisy dryer. I refitted the battery and pressed the on button. Nothing. Weirdly, I felt relief. No one could reach me. I didn't have to talk to anyone.

Now what?

Forty-one

I shoved my belongings back into my bag, even the broken phone and the positive pregnancy tester. Taking a deep breath, I pushed the door back out into the marketplace and left the toilets.

The market was busy. People milled about in a non-urgent fashion. They examined various artefacts and bits of tat on trestle tables before them: mildewed second-hand clothes on rails, dull copper and silver pots, homemade jewellery and jam. I marvelled at the calm faces around me. How could normal life be going on, whilst my world fell apart? Somehow, this made me feel better. For the first time that afternoon, I felt my thoughts clear and my fear lift.

So, I was pregnant. This was unexpected, but there must be thousands of girls and woman who found themselves in my shoes every single day? I was not going to accept more than half the blame for the pregnancy though. Why should I? It was true I shouldn't have drunk so much alcohol (and that I should have remembered the condoms in Mike's wallet), the same went for Mike, too. Even after that, we *both* could have sorted something out, but didn't. This was not just my mess, but his too. Whether Mike would accept that was another matter. Deep down, I guessed not. It wasn't like we had some amazing relationship to fall back on.

I broke away from the small crowd in the marketplace and wandered into the high street. I was unsure how long

I'd been in the toilets. Now it was mid-afternoon: the shadow cast from the town hall had moved ominously across the tarmac. So many windows were boarded up or smeared with whitewash. Depressing. I had been looking forward to getting out of this place! I felt ready for the change. I had outgrown my roots, I needed something more. I was being faced with a completely different change, one I had never considered before.

Did I want it?

Could I handle it?

What was 'for the best'?

I wondered what Mum and Dad would say. They hadn't been much older than I was now when they had me. I could see what was between them: us girls; a sense of shared history; mutual trust. My mother never worried where my father was, what he was doing or thinking. Even when he had been gone for months, she was always sure he would come back, which he always did. I used to get angry about this. I thought my mother was a doormat. Now I understood my father was a wanderer; he always had been and always would be. His sacrifice actually came in coming back to us, again and again. My mother's sacrifice was more involved: supporting us all, being there even when my father was not. But that was the path she had chosen. She hadn't *had* to stay with my dad. Like so many of my school friends' parents, she could have finished the relationship, become a true single mum. She had not.

Instead our curious family had thrived and continued, when many other more traditional families I had known had withered and died. If growing up had taught me anything, it was there was no 'right' way when it came to family and relationships.

'Whatever works.' Mum would say.

I'd heard her say that phrase so many times over the years. Usually Mum's friends came seeking her Yoda-style advice. Endless questions: 'What do I do when he won't go to bed at night?'; 'What do I do when she won't eat?'; 'What do I do when they backchat me?'

The answer was always the same: 'Whatever works'. I'd seen frustration in Mum's friends' eyes; I'd even privately thought Mum was copping out, instead of getting involved. I realised now what she'd meant: *try to do things the 'right' way... and you're destined for failure.*

I felt confident I could count on Mum and Dad's support. I was lucky. They would not throw me out or tell me I had brought shame on the family. My parents might have no money, but they stood by their kids no matter what. There would be disappointment and worry, though. I'd had big plans: I was supposed to be going to university in a matter of weeks. I'd wanted to have a career, move away, become independent.

If I kept the baby, could I still have the future I'd planned for?

If I chose not to have the baby, could I accept that and move on?

I turned a street corner. With a pang of guilt I realised I was just two streets away from Mike's. In a matter of seconds, I could go and tell him my news. But knowing Mike as I did, I knew he would not welcome the situation. I knew, as soon as I had seen the two lines on the positive tester stick, Mike and I were over. He and I had coasted along for too many months. We'd treated sex like a game without consequences. Well there were consequences. The game was over. I would have liked to make the decision with him, but with things the way they were between us, I knew that was not possible. I made a promise to Mike in my head, instead. He deserved to know the outcome of my decision when I had made it. I would stand by that.

From the streets I stared up at the clifftops, to the extravagant redbrick estate on top where Shona lived. Though I couldn't see her actual house, I fancied she might see me, ant-like, below. That was the way it had always been between us: Shona was the savvy one; the spoilt one; the one with all the answers. Just a few short months ago I would have run to her straight away, asking advice but really wanting her to tell me what to do. I knew I could not go to her now. There had been too many moments when I had let Shona take over. Over the years, we'd spent too many hours in trouble together, because of her. We'd stood outside classrooms and the headmaster's office; we'd even spent a whole night in a police cell, once after an underage Shona outside a pub had lightly pushed a policeman (he'd obviously had nothing else better to do than lock young girls up who were giving him beef). Worst though had been all the times I had known Shona was wrong, even if she hadn't … But I had gone along with what she wanted, anyway. I couldn't risk it. This was my decision to make. No one else could stand in for me and make it instead. Not even my oldest friend.

I found myself at the seafront in the blink of an eye, as if teleported there. My sisters and I had spent so many afternoons on the beach. I leaned on the railings, watching a lone boy and girl of about eight – twins perhaps – searching the shoreline with a bucket. They pulled various things from the tangled knots of seaweed the tide had left behind, the water far off in the distance. They collected shells, bits of rock smoothed by the waves, even a glass fishing buoy. I remembered doing the same with my sisters. I wondered when we stopped. I couldn't remember.

Their mother sat on the shale reading a book. Her jeans rolled up, her feet dangled in a rock pool. Despite it being high season, the donkeys were not tethered to the railings as they usually were. Their keeper must have taken them home early; it was a bad year and there were hardly any tourists about. The ice cream stall on the steps was deserted, its shutters down with CLOSED in bright red letters.

'I hate you!' The little girl said.

The kids' mother looked up from her book, but didn't intervene.

I saw the pain in the little boy's eyes, the trembling of his lip. I wondered if the little girl knew what she had said or the effect it could have. I remembered all the moments Sal had said the same to me. I'd stewed over it and hated her back, yet never said it. Maybe I should have? Maybe it was just a word.

'I hate you, too!' The little boy screeched.

'That's enough!' An adult voice cut through the air, silencing them. Their mum gaze settled on me and caught me looking. She smiled, self-conscious. 'Kids, hey?'

Embarrassed, I averted my eyes and moved on from the railings, towards the closed mini golf centre and the flashing lights of the open-fronted arcades. Inside, teenagers and the odd tourist sent money into penny falls machines and video games. A grinning boy of about seventeen managed to hook a teddy bear with a crane from another machine for his pale, much-younger girlfriend. He swore as it dropped back down, just inches from the chute.

'Rip off!' He smacked the glass with an open palm.

An alarm went off. Within seconds a security guard appeared from nowhere, escorting the still-arguing teen and the pale girlfriend from the premises.

Mum had always said parenthood was the hardest job of all, but I had just assumed it was something people just did. Mum made it look easy. I wondered if I could be like her, or whether I would just screw everything up? The media seemed to think no one could parent successfully without how-to websites, articles, books and programmes galore. I'd seen the feverish despair in various couple's eyes on television. They'd appeal to Supernanny and her many contemporaries as their families went wrong: 'Help us! Our children are running riot and our marriages are falling apart!' It always seemed to be those couples with the nice houses, large gardens, money in the bank. If they couldn't do it, how could I: a teenager, with no money and no home?

Yet at the same time, I could see what a nonsense that worry was too. My own mother hadn't had any of those things, either. There was no reason I could not be a good mother, as long as I took it seriously and thought my actions through. I could not rely on kneejerk fears to make my decision. I must weigh up every solution in the situation carefully if I was to choose the right one.

But what was the right one?

Forty-two

I stared at the notebook on the scarred Formica table. I had made my way back to Teddy's. I'd been scribbling for an hour, making lists. I found it soothed me. A milky coffee in a chipped mug had gone cold next to me: table rent. I stared at the list of options I had made. There were only two, really: I had the child – or I didn't. The more I considered both, the more complicated both scenarios became: a paradox.

Option 1: Abortion. This was a 'quick fix'. Things could go 'back to normal' in a matter of days, weeks at the most. I could go to university. Everything else I had planned would fall into place. The pregnancy would disappear into the past; a glitch in my otherwise smooth transition into adult life. For many girls, it would be that; it didn't make them bad people, either. I wondered whether I could do it. I did not just have the short term to consider, but the long term as well. I needed to be one hundred per cent sure. Would I be relieved? Or would I look back, with terrible regrets?

Option 2: Have the baby. If I did have the baby, I had to realise I would be a single mother. Even if Mike wanted to play a part in the baby's life (something I would be keen to encourage), I didn't believe I wanted him to have one in mine any longer. Babies didn't pull people together automatically; that's not what they were for. I needed to listen to my gut instinct, not hope for the best. *Look where that got us!* It was best if we drew a line under it, before we ended up hating each other. I didn't want to be a single mother. It hadn't been in my life plan (but then it probably wasn't in most women's). But Mike and I living together, getting married, being a family – all that 'expected' stuff - was out of the question. If 'whatever works' was key, then it would simply not work. Not for me. If Mike was truly honest with himself, not for him either.

There were so many other factors to consider, as well. Working would prove difficult, especially with childcare and public transport as poor as they were where I lived. Did I move away? What about my family, my support network? If I were to become a mother, what would become of my education? I had stuff I wanted to do, career stuff. Just because I had a child would not make ambitions go away. Why should they? How could I tell my child to follow their dreams if I had never followed mine? In fact, I needed to follow them all the more.

I knew there would be finger-pointing, too. Whether I had an abortion or kept the baby, people would feel it their right to tell me what I 'should' have done. Some would smugly tell me I was being responsible, having a termination; others would tell me I had murdered it, with disgust in their eyes. If I kept the child, I would be called a drain a society. The papers were always going on about pregnant teens and young mothers, suggesting the majority of them did it as a lifestyle choice to get benefits and council flats.

I smiled at the thought: *chance would be a fine thing*. Mums and babies ended up in bed and breakfasts instead for years, like Letty Welles did in year 11. Letty said the noise at the B&B was horrendous: her little boy, Jack, would cry for hours at the raised voices and the slamming of doors. Cigarette smoke filtered up from the communal gardens, infecting every room, so the air never felt clean. She and Jack had constant coughs and colds and there was never enough of anything: milk, food, peace. Some lifestyle choice!

I was outside again, but I didn't remember leaving Teddy's. Looking down the length of the long seafront, I saw the bright-coloured lights blink on, reflected in the tide as it came in. There was no sign of the boy and girl, or their mother. It was dusk. I could hear laughter coming from nearby pubs as drinkers spilled out into the beer gardens that overlooked the cove. I looked at my watch: nearly eight o' clock! Panicked, I realised the last bus was about to depart. I hitched my bag on my shoulder and ran.

The high street was deserted as my feet pounded the pavement: a ghost town, eerie and silent. I could hear my breath catch in my throat as I struggled to keep up with myself. I did not want to have to go to Mike's and ask him to drive me home, nor could I face Shona's interrogation. I didn't want to see either of them. Despite my reluctance to return earlier, I suddenly knew: I had to get home.

I needed to talk to Mum.

Forty-three

Racing through the marketplace, all the stalls were packed up: not one trader remained. The only soul in the vicinity was a drunk, slumped under the clock tower with a plastic bottle of cider. He gave me a gummy smile as I ran past, yelling something I couldn't catch.

I made it into the bus station to see the number 23 leaving the junction. Barely anyone was on board. The Driver refused to stop or open the doors as I ran alongside, banging on them. I couldn't hear his words above the grumbling noise of the engine, but from his gestures I knew he was swearing at me and telling me to get back. I was stopped, out of breath, a stitch in my side. I was forced to watch the bus sail out of the station and onto the link road. *Brilliant.*

Exhausted, annoyed and still panting for breath, I sat down on one of the graffittied benches in the bus station. I dug my phone out of my bag: the phone's screen was still blank and useless. I recalled reading somewhere that packing a waterlogged phone in unboiled rice sometimes does the trick in making them work again. I laughed at myself: I had much more important things to worry about than a dead phone. First up, how was I going to get home?

There was no guarantee Shona or her family would be in. I didn't want to drag myself up the cliff for nothing. Mike's house was closer, plus I could at least phone Mum from there. I'd have to wait for her to come and get me though, what if I cracked in the meantime and told him? Worse still, what if Mum couldn't come and get me? If Amanda or Sal were out, then there would be no one to look after the twins. Then I would be stuck with Mike all night. I might even talk myself out of breaking up with him! Since that was the only decision I had been able to make that day, I wanted to be able to hold on to it.

Thoughts racing, my gaze wandered over the empty bus station, towards the wall of payphones near the tourist information centre. On it were various faded posters for hotels, including The Belle View. Dad! There was Dad. He was bound to be at work. Perhaps I could stay with him, or he could take me back to Mum's in one of Pablo's vans? I grabbed a phone, shovelling some change in the slot.

In three rings, a bored Pablo answered. 'Hola.'

'Pablo, it's Lizzie. Lizzie Carmichael?' I said breathlessly.

'Yes, yes, what you want.' Pablo yawned. In the background, I could hear tinny muzak turned up too loud.

'I need to speak to my dad, please.' I crossed my fingers.

'Night off.' Pablo said. 'Back tomorrow for breakfast.'

With that, he hung up. I slammed the phone back in its handset, then slammed it a couple more times for good measure. *Typical!*

'Elizabeth Carmichael? Thought it was you. '

I turned, guilty. A young police officer in uniform stood in front of me. He wasn't much older than me, perhaps twenty-two: he had that look of someone just starting out. I didn't recognise him, but he seemed to know me.

'Yes?' I gulped, wondering if he was about to book me. 'Look, I was just annoyed. I didn't actually break the phone …?'

'We've been looking for you.' The police officer interrupted me. He smiled at me indulgently, like a grandfather would, despite his own young age.

'Looking for me?' I was confused. I wasn't a criminal on the run, why would they be looking for me?

'Yes, your parents were worried.' He laughed at the look on my face. 'They called your friends and your boyfriend, but no one had seen you. You said you'd be back hours ago. They couldn't get you on your phone, so we said we'd see if we could find you.'

Of course. One of the benefits of living in a small place was that everyone knew one another and did favours for them, like looking for AWOL teens.

'We'll give you a lift home.'

I nodded and followed him to a nearby police car. A female police officer sat in the front, in a neon jacket, visibly bored, clutching a Styrofoam cup. I did recognise her: she was Chloe Bensham's older sister, Matilda. I waved and Matilda gave me a little wave back. As I got in, the other police officer sat down heavily behind the wheel; he muttered something about me into the radio. There was a burst of static, then he turned the ignition on again.

Matilda smiled at me in the rear-view mirror and held up a bag of sherbet lemons. 'Want one?'

I took a sweet. 'How's Chloe?'

With a twinge of nostalgia, I realised I hadn't seen her in years: she hadn't gone to college with the rest of us. None of us had missed her, except perhaps Shona who'd always enjoyed picking on someone fatter than herself.

Matilda sucked on her sweet. 'Good. Really good, actually. She got a job as a nanny, working for a family up in London. Super-rich, you should see her room: she showed it to me on the webcam. Chloe reckons they even have one of those big American fridges that dispense ice cubes.'

I smiled. That sounded like Chloe. Chloe had always liked kids; I remembered she used to look after her little nephew – Callum? Caleb? – after school for her aunt. Chloe reckoned little kids were the most sensible people around;

they never got caught up in all the usual adult and teenage rubbish and never overcomplicated things. I could definitely see her point right now.

The police car sped into the night. Soon the streetlights in town had fallen away. There were only the cats' eyes in front of us and the yawning darkness of fields to either side of the vehicle. The only sounds were the engine, Matilda's rustling sweet wrappers and the occasional burst of static from the radio.

I settled back in my seat, the day's events still whizzing through my head. How did I break my news to my parents, my sisters? I supposed I just came out with it and braced myself. Sal would brand me an idiot for getting myself into the situation, but then, when hadn't she? Amanda might be a downer too. But my decision should not be based on how they might react. Sal and Amanda had their own lives: in just a couple of years Sal would be off to university. She'd never look back. I felt certain that Sal would be successful in everything she did; perhaps she'd even be happy. As for Amanda … No matter what she chose to do with her life, she would land on her feet. She always did!

The Policeman pulled the handbrake and said, 'Here we are.'

Home. Anxiety struck me again. I stared at the little cottage. The lanterns outside cast a sickly yellow glow on to the little river that travelled past the house. One year, we had tried to float in a tin bath we'd found, but it had sunk. Our makeshift boat sprang a leak, soaking our clothes. We'd all piled out, shrieking and laughing, blaming one another for being so fat. Mum had appeared on the doorstep with that crooked smile of hers. Both twins, still babies, hung on to her hip like furless koala bears.

'What are you all like!' She'd cackled like a witch.

Drawn by the lights of the police car and its engine, Mum appeared on the doorstep. Her face was pulled taut with worry. I could see Dad and the other girls in the living room through the window. None ventured out with Mum – probably because she'd forbidden them to.

'Thank you for bringing me back.' I said to the Police officer and Matilda, my eyes still fixed on Mum outside.

'You're welcome.' Matilda said.

She opened the door for me; I got out. I stood there a moment, hesitant. Mum had her arms folded around her thin frame, as if hugging herself. Her eyes were full of questions: *where had I been? What was going on? Was I okay?*

Words dried up in my mouth. Everything I had rehearsed abandoned me. I felt frustration, then anger: I was trying to be a grown up here! Behind us, the police car started up again, backing out of the driveway.

'I'm sorry.' I started crying.

Still bewildered, Mum had her arms around me seconds later. She cooed at me like I was a baby, telling me that whatever it was, it would be all right. I wanted to believe her, but suddenly the situation seemed too huge. It was beyond my control; it had run away with me. Dad stood helpless on the step, wondering if he should come out as well, yet knowing he had to keep the other girls at bay while I had my moment with Mum.

'I'm pregnant.' I spluttered.

Mum's reaction flickered across her face. Was that relief? Perhaps she had been expecting worse. I wondered briefly how it could be worse, then reminded myself it always could be. That was another of Mum's mantras, especially when us girls were complaining about having to clean our bedrooms, help around the house or clean out the cat's litter trays.

'I don't know what I want to do.' I admitted.

Mum smiled, touching her forehead against mine. 'Let's talk about it.'

Epilogue

I made my decision.

Mum and I talked for hours, on our own. The girls and Dad were banned. Sal's desperation to make me see her point of view included texting me from her bedroom, leading to Dad confiscating her phone. Hannah was also spotted attempting to see into the kitchen from the patio. Caught in the act, she pretended to be looking for Mum's alleged escaped cat (which was under the bed, like he always was).

Despite these interruptions, Mum and I were able to talk through all the elements that mattered: Mike. University. My future. Not once did Mum insist I consider her thoughts and feelings, though I asked her a couple of times. Each time she seemed to know I was asking her to lead me towards a conclusion.

'It's up to you.' She said.

There were barbed comments from Sal and a few incredulous questions from Amanda and Hannah. Mum and Dad batted these away for me, telling them it was my business, not theirs. (They ignored their shrieks that I was their sister and, of course, it concerned them!). I was grateful for Mum and Dad's support and understood my sisters were too young to really understand. Perhaps I wouldn't have, either.

The days that followed rattled past. It was only weeks later I really understood the consequences of my decision. The fear that had gripped me lessened; the anxiety had gone. I got the A Level results I was predicted but decided to defer my place at university for a year: not because I was afraid of going, but because I wanted to reassess the course, whether it was really what I wanted. I had begun to wonder if I had chosen it simply to 'get out' of Winby. Considering the fees and costs of university, I needed to be one hundred per cent sure it was the right choice. Instead, I took a job at a newsagent's in town. I read all their magazines and newspapers and scoured every prospectus of every university I was interested in.

Staying behind meant I had to wave off Shona and Mike. Shona went first, taking a ridiculous amount of baggage with her and even a hat stand. Her mum drove her to London in the Jaguar. I told Shona she should look up Chloe Bensham. Shona just smiled vaguely, not even remembering who Chloe was. Typical Shona. As she got in the car she told me she loved me and she'd be back every weekend. I knew she wouldn't.

Saying goodbye to Mike proved more difficult. We'd barely spoken in recent weeks. I had followed through on my promise and told him about the pregnancy. His reaction had been lukewarm at best, as I had predicted. When I told him of my decision and how I thought we should split up, his relief was obvious. I wasn't even hurt, I just wanted it all over with. We both knew the moment he got on the train to go to university, our relationship was officially over. Perhaps fear of the future made him wish it wasn't, because as I said goodbye, he suddenly hugged me.

'I love you.' He said.

I untangled myself and smiled. Tears had sprung up in the corner of my eyes, but I blinked them back. ''Bye Mike.'

Mike got on the train, his face a picture of puzzlement. I watched it pull out from the station.

Mum appeared on the platform next to me. 'You all right?'

'Fine.' I said, genuinely.

Travelling back to the house in the car with Mum, I looked out the window. I pretended to watch the passing fields, but really, I was considering my own reflection in the glass. Since regarding my stricken face in the aluminium mirror of those grotty toilets in town all those weeks ago, I finally felt at peace.

My decision was the right one.

For me.

THE END

Lightning Source UK Ltd.
Milton Keynes UK
UKHW01f0623170518
322697UK00001B/5/P

9 781999 855291